"An ethereal quality pervades the entire *Heartlight* narrative with a glowing core of hopefulness . . . it flows like a strong, smooth river in continuous dreamlike motion to a satisfying yet poignant conclusion . . . an excellent story."
—Brian Jacques

"*Heartlight* . . . crosses generational lines and becomes a vehicle for family discussions about love, death, independence, and integrity." —*Rocky Mountain News*

"What a joy to read. . . . the author manages to combine sophisticated concepts of physics with high fantasy in a marvelous way." —Madeleine L'Engle

"A splendid action-adventure science fantasy filled with deep, resonant emotional and spiritual undertones. . . . This books shines as a bold, original effort worthy of repeat readings." —*Publishers Weekly*

"Like Madeleine L'Engle, T. A. Barron very persuasively and very plausibly compounds great galactic adventure with questions fundamental to the universe—ours or any other." —Lloyd Alexander

"This thoughtful adventure combines fantasy, physics, and metaphysics in a manner reminiscent of Madeleine L'Engle." —*Booklist*

"A science-adventure fantasy in the best tradition of Madeleine L'Engle and C. S. Lewis. Barron's protagonists . . . . both exhibit the characteristics of real scientific champions: courage and competence, integrity and intelligence. " —Stephen H. Schneider,
Head of Interdisciplinary Climate Systems,
National Center for Atmospheric Research

turn the page for more rave reviews . . .

Praise for
Tree Girl

Praise for the *Lost Years of Merlin* series

The Lost Years of Merlin
An ALA Best Book for Young Adults
and a Texas Lone Star Award Winner

heartlight

T. A. BARRON

ACE BOOKS, NEW YORK

THE BERKLEY PUBLISHING GROUP
Published by the Penguin Group
Penguin Group (USA) Inc.
375 Hudson Street, New York, New York 10014, USA
Penguin Group (Canada), 90 Eglinton Avenue East, Suite 700, Toronto, Ontario M4P 2Y3, Canada
(a division of Pearson Penguin Canada Inc.)
Penguin Books Ltd., 80 Strand, London WC2R 0RL, England
Penguin Group Ireland, 25 St. Stephen's Green, Dublin 2, Ireland (a division of Penguin Books Ltd.)
Penguin Group (Australia), 250 Camberwell Road, Camberwell, Victoria 3124, Australia
(a division of Pearson Australia Group Pty. Ltd.)
Penguin Books India Pvt. Ltd., 11 Community Centre, Panchsheel Park, New Delhi—110 017, India
Penguin Group (NZ), 67 Apollo Drive, Rosedale, North Shore 0745, Auckland, New Zealand
(a division of Pearson New Zealand Ltd.)
Penguin Books (South Africa) (Pty.) Ltd., 24 Sturdee Avenue, Rosebank, Johannesburg 2196,
South Africa

Penguin Books Ltd., Registered Offices: 80 Strand, London WC2R 0RL, England

This is a work of fiction. Names, characters, places, and incidents either are the product of the author's imagination or are used fictitiously, and any resemblance to actual persons, living or dead, business establishments, events, or locales is entirely coincidental. The publisher does not have any control over and does not assume any responsibility for author or third-party websites or their content.

HEARTLIGHT

An Ace Book / published by arrangement with Philomel Books, a division of Penguin Group (USA) Inc.

PRINTING HISTORY
Philomel Books hardcover edition / September 1990
Ace mass-market edition / March 2003

Copyright © 1990 by Thomas A. Barron.
Cover art by Yvonne Gilbert.
Cover design by Judy Murello.
Text design by Kristin del Rosario.

ISBN: 978-0-441-01036-3

ACE
Ace Books are published by The Berkley Publishing Group,
a division of Penguin Group (USA) Inc.,
375 Hudson Street, New York, New York 10014.
ACE and the "A" design are trademarks belonging to Penguin Group (USA) Inc.

PRINTED IN THE UNITED STATES OF AMERICA

12 11 10 9 8 7 6 5 4 3

To Currie

contents

1

the mystery of the morpho

KATE spun around when she heard the crash.

"Cumberland!"

The golden retriever had Grandfather pinned on the kitchen floor. She dashed over and pulled the dog away, but not before he gave his victim one last slobbery kiss.

"Cumberland!" scolded Kate. "No jumping on Grandfather!"

"Nonsense," grumbled the old man as he painfully regained his feet. "I'm eighty years old and I've had a lot of practice falling. He's just keeping me in shape."

"Are you sure you're all right?"

Grandfather reached shakily for the arm of the rocker. He steadied himself, then slid into the seat. Pushing a tangle of white hair off his forehead, he glared at the dog.

"You will be the death of me, Cumberland."

The dog padded over to the chair and nuzzled his leg

affectionately. Heedless of any scorn, he assumed a dignified posture by the old man's side, his fur shining regally with the rust color of heather moors in autumn. Only his still-wagging tail revealed the irrepressible puppy underneath.

"Do you still feel like a picnic?" asked Kate.

Grandfather raised the great bushy brows that hung like clumps of wild moss over his eyes. "A picnic? Oh, dear—I did agree to that, didn't I?"

"It would be the first break you've taken from work in the last week," she coaxed.

He looked distractedly over his shoulder down the long hallway leading to his laboratory. "Could we put it off until tomorrow, Kaitlyn? I have so much to do just now."

"But, Grandfather . . . I've got everything all ready: cold chicken, carrot salad and two Granny Smiths. I even made you some lemon poundcake."

"Did you?"

"With Grandmother's recipe."

The white head cocked toward Cumberland, who was still briskly wagging his tail. "She is a terrible taskmaster, isn't she? I should be glad she doesn't own a whip." He looked up. "Although lemon poundcake is even more effective. I guess it would do me good to enjoy the garden colors at least once this year. Lord knows I need the break. And autumn in New England turns to winter so quickly."

Kate had already climbed atop a wooden stool and thrust her head into one of the deep cabinets built into the kitchen walls. Her muffled voice declared: "Drink some of that tea I made you, while I look for some plates. They must be in here somewhere." Pushing aside the jars of raspberry preserves her mother had made in August, she hunted for the stoneware she had eaten from so many times. "This kitchen has the deepest shelves! You could store an elephant in here."

"That's a farmhouse kitchen for you. Two hundred years ago, when this house was surrounded by nothing but wild woods and a few apple trees, those shelves had to hold all the provisions needed for a long winter."

"Now they hold mostly spider webs," said Kate, still searching for plates.

"Yes, I know. It's only thanks to your mother that this house has any food at all. If left to my own devices, I'd end up dining exclusively on books and prisms . . . with an occasional cup of tea to wash it all down."

Pouring a heavy dose of cream into his teacup, he reflected: "Sunshine and cream, that's all my mother said she ever required for a happy life. In Scotland she found plenty of good Jersey cream, but not much sunshine. Now here I am in America, with plenty of sunshine, but inferior cream."

As he took a sip, his eye caught a spiral-shaped prism, hanging from a string in the sunlight. Tiny fragments of rainbows swam across the wooden walls of the kitchen like shimmering fish of liquid light.

"You know," he said pensively, "a person's life should be like a prism: inhaling light . . . exhaling rainbows." He pushed back some stray strands of hair. "If only it weren't so brief. If only there were more time."

"Time for what, Grandfather?" asked Kate, descending from the cabinet with two handfuls of dust and spider webs, but no plates.

Grandfather didn't answer. Since moving to this quiet college town a year ago, Kate had been his constant companion, watching him do experiments in the lab, helping him mount butterflies for his collection, joining him for long walks in the university woods, or entertaining him with attempts to mimic his rich Scottish accent. Even before the move, when she had lived an hour away, she had enjoyed visiting Grandfather every bit as much as her schoolmates would enjoy going to the beach or the amusement park. Although she had always been something of a loner, the kids at her old school had seemed to accept that fact; they understood that she was more interested in her books and her collection of rocks and crystals than in the usual after-school games.

Now, however, life was different. Because her parents' appointments at the university—her father as chairman of the history department and her mother as a professor of geology—had caused them to move into town, a mere two blocks from Grandfather's house, Kate invariably came here straight after school. All the teasing she now had to endure about her "eighty-year-old boyfriend" made her angry, of course—enough to have broken the tooth of one especially loud-mouthed boy—and there were moments when she dearly wished she had never moved at all, or at least had some friends of her own age. But whenever she stepped through the door of Grandfather's house, those problems seemed to melt away. If Grandfather was preoccupied with an experiment, she would just curl up for the afternoon with one of his books on crystals, cloud formations, space travel, or Greek myths.

"Two peas in a pod." her mother had often called them. To which Grandfather invariably replied: "Two biscuits in a basket, if you please."

They were inseparable.

But not lately. For the last month or so, Grandfather had retreated deeply into his work, so deeply that even Kate's best efforts to rouse him had failed. He had always been a little absentminded, even during the years when he had been in charge of the Institute of Astrophysics. Yet now something was different. Even Cumberland sensed it. Most painful of all, Grandfather had taken to locking the lab door at all times, and he wouldn't—or couldn't—open it when she knocked.

"You are feeling all right, aren't you? No more of those dizzy spells?"

"Of course not, dear child. I'm fit as a fiddle."

Trying not to sound overly interested, Kate asked: "Then what's been keeping you from answering the door to the lab? What is it you're working so hard on?"

The old man drew in a thoughtful breath. "It's complicated," he finally replied. He scratched behind Cumberland's long ears. "Too complicated."

"Is it another telescope?" she asked. "Like the huge one you built in South America?"

"No, Kaitlyn. Designing that telescope was exciting, but not really my normal line of work." His face creased slowly into a smile. "I did enjoy those trips to Chile, though. I used to do some of my best butterfly collecting en route to the Southern Observatory."

Kate continued to probe the cupboards for plates. "Another laser, then? You're inventing a new one?"

A sparkle from the prism flashed in Grandfather's eyes. "No, not another laser. That would be a much simpler task." He resumed rocking the chair, as if for a moment he had forgotten Kate was there.

She leaned across the counter. "Grandfather, do your

experiments have something to do with traveling faster
than light?"

Grandfather stopped rocking, and his eyebrows lifted
high on his forehead. "How did you ever—"

"The pamphlet in your bookshelf," replied Kate. "It's
your most recent one, so I thought it might be what
you're working on."

"Don't ever tell me you're not a budding scientist,"
nodded the old astronomer.

"But I'm *not*. You know I almost flunked science!"
Kate looked at her feet. "I just miss you, that's all."

"Miss me? But I'm right here. I haven't gone any-
place."

"Oh, yes you have!" Kate's eyes began to brim with
tears. "You've been so buried in your mysterious project
for the last month I've hardly seen you! Right after
school started, something happened to you. All of a sudden. It's like—why, it's like you took off to another
planet."

Grandfather stiffened. "I suppose I have been a little
distracted lately."

Kate tossed her blond braid over her shoulder. It
reached almost to her jeans, which not so long ago had
drooped about her legs like wide pantaloons. Now they
pinched her uncomfortably, like so many of her clothes.
So much had changed during the past year, and her jeans
were the least of it. New home, new school, new braces
. . . The only thing that hadn't changed, she used to tell
herself, was her friendship with Grandfather: Nothing
could ever change that.

"I've tried not to disturb you," she continued. "I've
really tried! Mom and Dad keep saying it's just a project
you're doing, and all projects have to end sometime. But

I'm getting tired of waiting! I don't have anybody to talk to now except Cumberland! Sometimes . . . sometimes I wish you weren't a famous astronomer, with a dozen projects always on your mind!"

The old man beckoned and Kate stepped slowly to the side of the rocking chair. Kneeling, she rested her head against his familiar white lab coat. As his arms enfolded her, she closed her eyes and tried to swallow the lump in her throat.

"I'm sorry, Grandfather! I just miss you."

"I'm the one who's sorry, Kaitlyn. I've been so wrapped up in my work I haven't remembered anything else."

Suddenly, something wet and scratchy slapped Kate's face.

"Cumberland!" She struggled to push the dog away, but he continued to lick her hands and arms and even the air when he could no longer reach her face.

"Down, Cumberland!" commanded Grandfather, his eyes twinkling. "You never miss a chance for a bit of affection, do you?"

The great retriever swished his broad tail in agreement.

Grandfather turned to the girl kneeling by his chair. "It's a great blessing for me that your parents got teaching positions right here at the university."

"For me, too. I'd rather spend time here than anywhere else. It's better than school, that's for sure." She glanced at the cupboard. "Now, let's eat. I'm hungry! Where *do* you keep your plates these days? I can't find them anywhere."

"I think they're all in the lab," came the sheepish reply. "I guess I've let things get a little disorganized around here in the past few weeks."

"So what do you use for a plate when you're in the kitchen?"

Grandfather pointed guiltily to a tottering wooden chair in the corner. On it was a half-eaten cheese sandwich, sitting inside an old Frisbee.

"Yikes!" Kate exclaimed. "If Mom knew you were eating out of a dirty old Frisbee, she'd be over here in ten seconds with a truckload of new dishes."

"No doubt," agreed Grandfather. "But let's not ruin her day by telling her, all right?"

Sometimes Kate felt Grandfather needed a mother more than she did. She grinned. "All right, I won't tell."

"Now let's have that picnic. I want to try some of your famous lemon poundcake."

"Without any plates?"

"I have an idea," Grandfather suggested, lowering his voice to a whisper, as if he were about to impart a valuable scientific secret. "How about this: Let's *both* eat out of the Frisbee. Just this once." He touched her nose gently as he rose from the rocker and walked over to an oaken table piled high with various papers and journals of astronomy and physics. Opening a drawer beneath it, he pulled out a faded cotton tablecloth printed with green and purple flowers. He regarded it affectionately before laying it over his forearm. Kate knew it had once belonged to Grandmother.

"Take your sweater, Kaitlyn. The sun is out, but there's an autumn chill in the air already. We may get our first frost tonight."

*　　*　　*

ARMS laden with picnic makings, the old man and the girl stepped down the flagstone walk to the garden. Close behind them followed Cumberland, his tail wagging energetically.

Kate used her shoulder to push open the old wooden gate, and Cumberland strolled through immediately, rubbing her leg as he passed. Then came Grandfather, moving more stiffly than usual, it seemed to her. His eye was on a patch of unruly grass next to the great stone fountain, but before he could speak, Kate had already put down her load at the very spot.

Grandfather shook open the picnic cloth and set it carefully on the grass. Grape arbors, hanging heavily with Concord bunches, sent the fragrance of their fermenting fruit in all directions. Shafts of purple aster grew tall and proud, the better for being untended by gardening hands. A few milkweed stalks, their seed pods full and ripe, stood like streetlamps amidst the fallen leaves surrounding the old maple. Most glorious of all were the chrysanthemums, which decorated the garden with a full array of autumn colors.

"I've never seen the mums so beautiful," said Kate, patting down the cloth.

"My favorites are the purple ones. Chrysanthemums are usually gone by now. It's rare they last into October, but this year the frost has been kind to them." He sighed wistfully. "It doesn't seem so long ago that your grandmother first planted them here. She had a long wooden box filled with roots and took great care to plant each one individually, letting it know it was specially appreciated. I'm afraid I haven't been doing my garden chores very well since she died . . . There won't be any daffodils, tulips, or hyacinths next spring."

He looked back at the garden gate, swinging slowly in the breeze. "There is no better place than a garden to see the changing of the seasons, Kaitlyn. Birth, death, then rebirth, all happen naturally, regularly, and peacefully. Flowers don't fight against death like people do."

He submerged in thought for a moment, then cast an eye toward Kate, his voice a whisper. "This was her favorite spot to sit, you know."

"I know, Grandfather." Kate wanted to reach over and hug him, but held herself back. She added gently: "This was her favorite tablecloth, too. I hope she wouldn't mind our using it for a picnic."

"She wouldn't mind. She used it for quite a few picnics herself."

Together, in silence, they unpacked the meal. Cumberland positioned himself nearby, his brown eyes filled with longing for a taste of lemon poundcake.

They ate quietly in the crisp autumn air. Every so often Grandfather's misty eyes would glint in the sunlight. He seemed to be remembering other places and times, and Kate did not want to disturb him. Some of their best conversations, Grandfather had once observed, happened without any words at all. Often one of them would finish the other's sentence; just as often, the sentence wasn't even started and the other understood.

Nobody else but Grandfather made Kate feel so comfortable—just as she was, braces and all. Nobody else but Grandfather welcomed her endless questions (usually inspired by her forays into his vast collection of books)—unless, of course, he was in the middle of an experiment, in which case even an earthquake couldn't distract him. To Grandfather it made no difference whether she asked about how the universe began or how the penny-farthing bicycle got its name: Both questions deserved an answer. One day last winter, a simple query about the formation of snow-flakes prompted Grandfather to lead her outside in a raging snowstorm, where they caught the falling crystals on their gloves and talked about the endless variety until their numbed feet finally forced them to go back indoors. Rather often, it seemed, she would raise a question that even Grandfather couldn't answer. At those moments, his bushy brows would climb skyward and he would reply: "Only God knows the answer to that one, Kaitlyn. But if you keep asking, perhaps He'll give us a hint."

Of course, having a famous astronomer as a grandfather wasn't always peaches and cream. Grandfather's image often haunted her at school, whether from the other kids' teasing or from her tendency to daydream during class. Only last week, she hadn't been listening when Mrs. Donovan, her seventh-grade science teacher, had assigned a special overnight homework project. When Kate arrived the next morning empty-handed, her classmates made great sport of her. Somebody slipped a small dunce cap into her book bag; somebody else taped a sign to the end of her braid that read: "Pull here to wake."

Mrs. Donovan, who had a figure like an overstuffed shopping bag, took her out to the hallway. Shaking her head solemnly, she said: "Kate, Kate, Kate! You have no idea how hard I've tried to get you to show some interest in my science class! With no success at all, I'm afraid. At first I thought it was just a matter of time, but now—now I've given up. Don't you share any of your grandfather's interest in science?"

Kate didn't respond. Answering such questions only made things worse.

"Really, Kate! How can someone with a family like yours be so lazy in school?"

She merely gazed at the floor.

Placing her hands on her nonexistent hips, Mrs. Donovan declared: "If you think having a famous grandfather allows you to daydream through my classes, I've got bad news for you."

"I wasn't daydreaming!" Kate objected. "I was thinking."

Mrs. Donovan peered dubiously down at her. "Thinking about what?"

Kate hesitated. "I was thinking about sunspots—how they form, how they can even change our weather. I'm reading about them in one of Grandfather's books."

The teacher scowled, her several chins drooping in unison like a stack of frowns. "For someone who daydreams her way through school, you certainly do come up with some inventive excuses."

"I wasn't daydreaming!" protested Kate, her temper flaring like a solar prominence.

Grandfather never asked, nor did Kate explain, why she came home from school so early that day.

"Do you remember your grandmother, Kaitlyn?"

Grandfather's question jolted her back to the present. "Yes, sort of. I mean, it was a long time ago that she died."

"Not so long, really." He glanced at the grape arbor. "She knew me, Kaitlyn. She knew that I much preferred the wild moors over any garden, that I missed the call of the curlew, the crumbling stone walls, the gorse growing wild that I knew as a child in Scotland. The moors

are in my blood. If she'd left it up to me, this garden
would look more like the Back of Beyond!" He laughed,
remembering some distant moment. "But she taught me
how to love a calmer place like this, as well as some of
the wilder places within myself. Your grandmother
could see further through a millstone than most." He
sighed. "The only thing she couldn't teach me was how
to accept the fact of death. That lesson has always been
beyond my grasp, I'm afraid. She went so peacefully
when her time came . . . while I'm certain I'll battle it
every step of the way."

Kate thought about the large portrait of Grandmother
as a young woman that hung in the hallway by the front
door. Those deep brown eyes, the open face, the comfortable dignity of her posture, all made her seem so
alive. And so lovely. There was also a slight touch of
impatience at the corners of her mouth: It was clear she
would much rather have been out working in the garden
than sitting still for a formal portrait. Like Kate, she
often wore her flowing blond hair in a braid, but unlike
Kate's slapdash knotting, it always looked effortlessly
elegant. To have known such a person, and then to have
lost her . . .

"She would have liked to have known you better," he
continued. "The two of you would have much in common."

Kate flushed with doubt. "I don't know. She was so
wise and beautiful and everything."

"You don't think you're wise?"

"Are you kidding? Just ask Mrs. Donovan! I'm at the
bottom of my class."

Grandfather shook his white mane. "Einstein was
bored at school, too."

"That's different! He was a big brain! I'm more like a big dunce."

"A dunce is one thing you're most definitely not, my child. You have very special gifts. You have extraordinary insights. It's only a matter of time before you discover how you want to use them. Try to be patient—"

"Patient! I've never been patient in my life!"

"I said *try* to be patient, Kaitlyn." He extended a weathered hand to her. "This has been a hard year for you, hasn't it?"

Kate nodded, and her round eyes began to fill with tears. "Sometimes I wish we'd never moved! I don't have a single friend at school. Everybody's always making my life miserable."

He drew her near in a gentle hug. "You're still my special friend, you know. You're the same little girl I've always loved."

"But I'm not!" she spouted, pushing away. "I'm not little! And I'm not the same! Nothing's the same!" Her gaze fell to the ground. "Sometimes I feel like . . . like I don't belong *anywhere*!"

"Kaitlyn," said Grandfather quietly. "You still belong here."

She looked at his eyes, sparkling in the same hazel-green hue as her own, and felt her tears welling to the surface. She buried her head in his familiar white lab coat.

For many minutes, Grandfather held her and said nothing. Gently he stroked her long braid, as the sound of her quiet sobbing filled the garden. Cumberland nestled his head between his paws.

In time, Kate lifted her face.

"Oh, Grandfather . . . this was supposed to be a fun picnic for you."

"Who says this isn't fun?" he answered with a twinkle. "I thought you were just working up an appetite for some lemon poundcake."

Kate wiped her face on her sleeve. "Grandfather, I don't know what I'd do without you."

"You'd probably eat off clean dishes, like normal people."

Kate grinned, already feeling a little better. "Somehow you always—oh! Look!"

She jumped to her feet, pointing to a tiny glittering form dancing on the fountain. "There! What an amazing butterfly!"

Grandfather, too, was on his feet. *"Morpho nestira,"* he said softly in wonderment. "So you are still alive."

As the butterfly settled upon the stone fountain, it began slowly to open and close its delicate wings, rhythmically, like a beating heart. Each time the wings opened, they flashed with iridescent blue, green, and violet—colors more brilliant than Kate had ever seen. As the wings drew closer together, the colors evolved from the deepest hues into an opalescent luster. The undersides of the wings, by contrast, were a simple shade of brown, with only a subdued pearly sheen around the edges providing any hint of the colors inside. Then suddenly: The wings reopened in a burst of brilliance, radiating blues and greens of impossible purity.

"Those wings are like rainbows," Kate whispered.

"Yes," answered Grandfather, "but even better. No rainbow has colors so intense. Those wings are covered with millions of microscopic prisms that concentrate and purify the light."

"What did you call it?"

"*Morpho nestira*. It comes from South America."

"South America! How did it get up here?"

Grandfather watched the pulsing wings thoughtfully.
"I brought it back with me, on my last trip to the Southern Observatory in June. It took me three expeditions
into the Amazon to find one. At the rate the forests down
there are being destroyed, the butterflies' habitat is being
wiped out and they may soon be extinct."

"You wanted it for your collection?"

"No. Not this butterfly."

"Then why did you bring it back here?"

"I wanted to study its wings. How they move. How
they refract light. How they *glow*. Kaitlyn, the wings of
the morpho butterfly produce the purest colors found
anywhere on Earth."

For a split second, Kate turned from the butterfly to
glance at Grandfather. His eyes shone with the excitement of discovery; he was utterly immersed in the present. This was the Grandfather she knew.

"No technology ever invented can do what those
wings can do," he continued. "What the morpho uses
every day to frighten predators or signal courtship is
really the nearest thing to *pure light* found on this
planet."

At that instant, the butterfly lifted off from the fountain. It rose into the air and then, with a sparkling swoop,
fluttered in the direction of the chrysanthemums. For a
moment it danced above the colorful petals, and then,
whirling, floated slowly toward the picnickers. It hesitated for an instant, as the ocean sun hesitates on the
horizon before setting, then landed softly on Kate's forearm.

Her heart pounded as she watched the rhythmic opening and closing of the wondrous wings. Not daring to
move, nor even to breathe, she felt a warm tingling sensation bathing her entire body. When the tiny legs of the
butterfly shifted slightly, she could feel the pressure of
each footstep on her skin, even through her heavy
sweater. In that moment, time stood still. The universe
became a suffusion of colors—brilliant, flashing colors
flowing from boundless blues to radiant greens and vi-
olets. Grandfather was right: No rainbow could possibly
compare with these radiant wings.

Finally, the butterfly stirred, and the glittering wings
carried it skyward. Gracefully, it rode a breeze over the
garden fence and out of sight. Kate quietly reached for
Grandfather's hand. Silently, they stood for several
minutes, looking at the spot where the morpho had disappeared.

"Its wings are more than just colors," said Kate at last.
"You know what I mean?" She wasn't quite sure herself
what she meant.

"I think so," replied the white-haired man beside her.
"Those wings are *light*, Kaitlyn. Pure light."

"That's why they glow so much?"

Grandfather nodded. "And they'll continue to glow
like that as long as the butterfly remains alive."

"Alive?"

His face grew somber. "Something changes when the
butterfly dies. The wings grow dimmer, duller. The
prisms still refract light, but it's only a pale imitation of
the living morpho."

"Why?" demanded Kate. "What happens when it
dies?"

"That, I'm afraid, is still a mystery."

"Is that why you wanted to study it? Why you brought it all the way back here?"

"Not exactly. Let's just say the wings of the morpho hold many great mysteries. When my experiments were done, I couldn't bear to let it die in some little glass case in the lab. So I let it go, out here in the garden. That was over a month ago."

"That's a long time for a butterfly."

"Yes," replied Grandfather, again suddenly distracted. "And quite a month it's been." His brow wrinkled in concern, and he released her hand. "Time for me to get back to work, Kaitlyn."

He pushed the remains of the lemon poundcake toward Cumberland. Before he could remove his hand, the dog snapped up the entire serving in one bite.

"What did you learn from the morpho's wings?" pressed Kate. "Please tell me."

The white eyebrows lifted. "Something I never dreamed possible."

"About light, Grandfather?"

"That's how it began. But . . ."

"But what?" pressed Kate. "Tell me, please."

The aging astronomer pushed back a handful of white hair, then gazed at her for a long moment. At last, he spoke softly, so softly that she could barely hear. "One day, Kaitlyn, if I'm right, what I learned could make it possible for people to travel to the most distant stars in the universe."

Kate's gaze fell. "I guess that means you're going to lock yourself up in the lab again."

"I'm afraid so," answered Grandfather. "I'm sorry, Kaitlyn. I hope it won't be much longer. I'm really very close." He reached out his hand and gently raised her chin. "But I'd love to join you for supper."

She lifted her eyes. "Really?"

"Yes, Kaitlyn." A warm smile illuminated his face and he drew a deep, satisfied breath. "I needed this picnic more than you know."

"So did I," Kate replied. "More than you know."

Although something about Grandfather still troubled Kate—something she couldn't quite put her finger on—his promise made her happier than she had felt in weeks. She glanced at the spot on her forearm where the morpho had rested, then turned back to Grandfather. "You'd better get going. The sooner you start, the sooner you'll finish! Cumberland and I will clean things up."

The old man winked at her. "At least you don't have any plates to wash."

2

almighty wings

BY ten o'clock, Grandfather still had not emerged from behind the locked door of the lab. Kate finally gave up waiting and prepared dinner for Cumberland and a ham and cheese sandwich for herself. Just in case, she made an extra one for Grandfather.

She had barely taken her first bite when the telephone on the kitchen counter rang. She put down the sandwich and lifted the receiver.

"Hi, Mom," she said through a mouthful of ham and cheese. "I was going to call you, really I was."

"I know, dear. Sometimes you're just as absent-minded as your grandfather, that's all. It's a Prancer family trait. Are you coming home?"

"It's a weekend, so I was hoping to stay over here tonight. Is that all right?"

"Well . . ."

"Please?"

"Grandfather certainly needs the company these days. I'm worried he's working too hard—especially the past few weeks. All this pressure isn't good for him."

Kate knew well the edge in her mother's voice. Grandfather's health was something the family understood was a problem, but never discussed openly. She volunteered: "We had a great picnic out in the garden this afternoon." She didn't add that Grandfather had promptly locked himself in the lab again.

"All right, Kate. You can stay."

"Thanks, Mom."

"Goodnight, dear. Don't stay up too late."

Taking her sandwich with her, Kate stepped over to the rocker and opened *Pennington's Exotic Butterflies*, which had been her afternoon reading, to the page about morphos. A pair of lustrous wings, poised to lift off from the page, greeted her as before. Next to the picture, written in Grandfather's nearly illegible scrawl, were the words *light and soul*.

Just then she heard a loud sizzling and crackling, like frying bacon but much louder, coming from behind the locked door to the lab. A strange burning smell floated down the long hallway from the lab to the kitchen. *If only I had X-ray vision*, thought Kate.

Hearing no further sound, she scanned the bulging shelves of Grandfather's book collection, which lined both sides of the hallway and one entire wall of the kitchen. She particularly loved this part of the rambling old house. The oaken shelves of Grandfather's library held at least fifty books on the nature of light, and twice that number on the evolution of stars. A particular star named Trethoniel was the subject of so many volumes that it required a special shelf all its own. Kate's favorite

books were about the weather, its many patterns and
causes; the little ladder was still resting in front of that
particular section. She smiled at seeing the large number
of works bearing the name *Miles Prancer, D. Phil.* She
knew from experience that these were beyond her comprehension, except for the dedications, which were always to Grandmother and always loving without being
sentimental.

Then she spied a small gray pamphlet leaning against
the most recent edition of Grandfather's text, *The Life
Cycle of Stars.* It looked innocuous, even uninteresting,
except for its title: *Beyond Starships: Is It Possible to
Travel Faster Than Light?* Protruding from the pamphlet
was a badly crumpled piece of paper. It looked like a
letter that had been thrown away and later retrieved.

She hesitated for an instant, then removed the letter
and read it to herself.

THE ROYAL SOCIETY
London
Founded 1662

My Dear Prancer:

*It is with considerable regret that I must report
that the Royal Society has elected to withdraw its
invitation to you to present your most recent specu-
lations about traveling faster than light. Given our
increasingly crowded calendar, we are simply unable to schedule a time to consider your ideas, intriguing though they may be to some of our
members.*

Please rest assured that this decision was taken

*only after the most thorough deliberation. Should
you choose to present a paper at some time in the
future, presumably on a subject rising to traditional
standards of documentation and proof, we would of
course be pleased to consider your application.*

> *Yours Cordially,*
> *Rt. Hon. M. L. Hunter*
> *Chairman, Committee on Peer Review*

Suddenly, Kate felt something move behind her.

She spun around, dropping the letter. But there was
nothing unusual to be seen. Cumberland had gone outside after his meal, so she was completely alone.

Yet, it was almost as if she could feel the presence of
something else in the kitchen. Something shadowy . . .
and cold . . . and watching.

Cautiously, she crept closer to the stone fireplace. "It's
nothing, I'm sure," she told herself. "Probably just a
draft from the chimney." She knew the kitchen fireplace
was so old it was like an open window.

As she bent over to look up the chimney, the ceiling
light flickered noisily. She froze, as the light sputtered
and wavered on the edge of going out.

Again she sensed something behind her and she
whirled around. Her heart was pounding. Where is Cumberland? What had Grandfather once said about hearing
ghosts in this house, moaning and creaking with the
wind in these old timbers? The light flickered again, like
a candle in a cold breeze.

Slowly, Kate backed up until she was pressed against
the wall of books. She stood there, too afraid to scream.

*   *   *

"ALMOST . . . almost there," Grandfather muttered as he pored over a gleaming green metal box, surrounded by a gnarled nest of wires and silicon chips. "I'm so close now I can taste it."

As if he were gathering his strength for the final moment, he lifted his eyes from the green box and surveyed the familiar surroundings of his lab. In addition to the thirty-centimeter telescope poised beneath the sky-hatch, the room contained a powerful microscope, an ultraviolet spectrograph, a radiometer specially designed to measure stellar luminosity, and several homemade lasers. One solid-state laser, only as large as a lemon, sat on a small freezer capable of chilling microchips nearly to absolute zero. A stack of homemade holograms rested on his cyclic interferometer, still showing the measurements of its last light wave.

The walls were cluttered with star maps and computer-enhanced images of various celestial bodies, as well as Grandfather's Oxford University diploma, now so faded with age that most of its Latin script was indecipherable. Next to it was posted a piece of yellow paper with the words, written in crayon several years ago: "Dear Grandfather, Thank You For The Pretty Butterfly. Love, Kate."

In the far corner stood a new invention: a large device designed to measure the health and longevity of stars. Right now, it was clattering relentlessly as it analyzed some recent data on the Sun.

The lone bookshelf in the lab was tilting dangerously; it contained mostly notebooks of many colors and thicknesses. The only exceptions were tattered copies of the *Old* and *New Testaments* (King James Version), *The Once and Future King*, and *The Wind in the Willows*.

(Aristotle's collected writings, sometimes also found there, were currently being employed as a lamp stand.)

Next to the bookshelf, directly beneath the lab's open window, stood his bureau of butterflies, holding thirty-five specimens in each of its eighteen slim drawers. Against one side were piled several nets, jars, and other trappings of lepidopterology; on its top, an unfinished chess game waited patiently for someone to make the next move. Carefully placed on the windowsill were a plaster cast of a polar bear paw print and a fossil of a trilobite. Next to them rested a small stack of dinner plates, permanently bound together with the glue of petrified cheese sandwiches.

Leaning precariously against the wall, a large wooden table sagged beneath the weight of hundreds of specialized tools, prisms, cannisters, and components—so many that not even Grandfather could remember what all of them were meant for. His portraits of Albert Einstein, Leonardo da Vinci, and Robert H. Goddard, once in clear view, were now totally obscured by the rising tide of clutter on the table.

Grandfather's gaze returned to his desk, and to the green metal box resting atop his minicomputer. The surface of the box shone with an electric luster and it vibrated, humming faintly, like the voice of a Tibetan monk chanting a mantra. Behind the minicomputer, a crowded rack of beakers and flasks, filled with brightly colored liquids, rattled continuously from the vibration of the green box.

"Almost," he whispered, perspiration gathering in the wild eyebrows on his forehead. "Steady now. Steady . . ."

Concentrating intently, he adjusted several of the

wires and silicon chips protruding from the box, using
a slender pair of tweezers. But for the occasional pause
to check a formula on his clipboard or punch a few keys
on the minicomputer, Grandfather worked without in-
terruption until, at last, he heaved a sigh that had been
building for more than fifty years.

"Ah, yes," he whispered, placing the tweezers on a
stack of computer printouts next to his desk.

His hands trembling, Grandfather removed several
wires and closed the lid of the green box. Then, with an
excited gleam in his eye, he pushed the key on the minicomputer marked *Enter*.

He sank back in his chair, feeling strangely drained,
at a moment when he had always imagined he would
feel triumphant. Wearily, he raised his wrinkled hands
before his face and regarded them ruefully. How quickly
the time had flown since those hands had first thrown a
baseball or toyed with a telescope . . .

Then he turned again to the green box, and his energy
started to return. "It's here," he said softly. "My moment
in the Sun is finally here."

"Grandfather!"

At first he thought he had just imagined the cry. Then
it came again, this time louder than before.

"Grandfather!"

Someone began battering on the door to the lab.

"Kaitlyn!" he exclaimed. "What on Earth are you yell-
ing about?"

He swiftly covered the green box with a ragged cloth,
then walked over to the door. He turned the latch and
started to open it—when suddenly a violent push shoved
both him and the door aside.

"Oh, Grandfather!" she cried, running to him and hugging him tightly. "Grandfather, I'm scared!"

The old man knelt down and peered into her frightened eyes. She was quivering with fear. "What is it, Kaitlyn? What happened?"

"There's—there's something here in the house, Grandfather! Something like—like a ghost. I'm sure of it. I felt it."

Grandfather drew her close and stroked her long braid. "I'm sure you did, my child. This is an old house, and sometimes it does strange things."

Kate pushed herself away. "No, but this was real! I'm sure! I'm not just imagining things." She glanced behind herself at the open door to the hallway. Nothing looked at all unusual; the hallway now seemed quiet, even inviting.

Kate swallowed hard and started to continue—when suddenly she noticed the strangely contented look on the old astronomer's face. "Grandfather, what is it?"

The lab was dim, lit only by the shaded table lamp next to the desk, but the sparkle in Grandfather's eyes was unmistakable. "If there are any ghosts in this house tonight, dear child, they must be good ones."

"What do you mean?"

Pushing back a handful of white hair, he answered: "I mean that I have just made a breakthrough that has taken me more than fifty years to accomplish."

"Is this the project you told me about after the picnic?"

"Yes, Kaitlyn." A sudden recollection clouded Grandfather's face and he added: "Oh, I missed our date for supper, didn't I? Sorry about that."

"That's all right." Slowly, Kate's concerns about ghosts were being overcome by curiosity. "Go on,

Grandfather. Tell me about this breakthrough."

Stiffly, Grandfather stepped across the floor to his desk. "Ever since I was a student at Oxford, I have suspected that deep in the core of every star there is a special substance—a substance that holds the key to explaining how stars really function."

"Isn't that the stuff you've written so much about? The stuff you call PLC?"

"PCL," corrected Grandfather. "It stands for *Pure Condensed Light.*"

Kate nodded, but her attention had focused on the ragged cloth covering something on the minicomputer. A mysterious humming sound, accompanied by the constant rattling of beakers, seemed to come from beneath the cloth.

"Of course," continued Grandfather, "that was only a theory. There was no way I could prove that PCL actually exists—let alone that it might also have some rather peculiar properties."

"Like traveling faster than light?"

"Yes, Kaitlyn." The old man's eyes shone like beacons. "It won't be long before I will unveil a discovery that will one day make spacecraft obsolete. At last, PCL's existence will finally be treated as a fact, and my own maligned reputation will be restored." His eyes darkened. "Most people allow themselves to be herded around like sheep, I'm afraid, in science just as much as in religion or politics. They prefer a daily dose of predictable rules—with a touch of self-righteousness—to the often unpredictable truth. So the general opinion that I've been wrong about PCL hasn't really bothered me. But, in recent years, even my closest colleagues have started to doubt my sanity, and that's hurt a bit."

"Is that why they wouldn't let you speak to their meeting?" asked Kate, taking her eyes from the cloth and studying Grandfather sympathetically. "That's the rudest thing I ever heard of."

A half-smile creased the astronomer's face. "You read the Royal Society letter, didn't you?"

Kate nodded guiltily.

"That's all right. I should never have kept it anyway. Couldn't throw it away for some reason. But the last laugh is going to be mine."

"I still don't understand why they'd treat you that way. Why do they hate you so much?"

"They don't hate me. They're just frightened."

"What's so frightening about traveling faster than light?"

Grandfather laughed. "What's so frightening? Nothing at all, except that it could alter the whole way we think about the universe! It could destroy hundreds of old theories and build new bridges between relativity and quantum mechanics that now seem impossible."

"I still don't think they should have treated you like that," objected Kate. "If you ask me, the Royal Society is a bunch of royal jerks!"

"Old Ratchet would have agreed with you," replied Grandfather. "He used to fondly call them 'brain-dead Neanderthals.' " He turned to a dusty photograph on the wall of a thin, hairless man in a wheelchair. "Ah, Ratchet! If only you were still around to witness this moment! You never doubted that PCL exists, or that it powers the energy of every star, although I doubt that even you realized what *other* powers it might also have." Grandfather chortled to himself. "Perhaps it's for the best you're not still here. I don't think you could stand the idea that I—someone you saw as your lowly student—crossed the finish line before you did."

Kate remembered well the mysterious saga of Dr. Ratchet, which she had heard so often from Grandfather. Suffering from a degenerative nervous disease, which had struck him in his thirties and left him confined to a wheelchair for the rest of his life, Ratchet had developed an amazing ability to perform four-dimensional mathematics in his head. Ultimately he came to rely heavily on Grandfather, his best student, to translate his visionary theories into practice, which is why the young Miles Prancer had first trained his telescope on the little-known star called Trethoniel. Despite his genius, however, Ratchet remained an embittered and angry man, haunted always by the fear of death. He never missed an opportunity to berate a colleague or squash a student. Consequently, few tears were shed when he died in a mysterious fire that destroyed Oxford's entire physics complex and left behind little more than the scorched wreck of his wheelchair.

"So you've finally proved that PCL exists?" asked Kate.

"Even better," answered Grandfather, and his eyebrows lifted like rising white clouds. "I have identified all of its ingredients. I now possess the recipe for PCL."

"Wow!" exclaimed Kate. "But how?"

"Perseverance, Kaitlyn. That's how. If there is any quality I wish for you, it's perseverance." With a swipe of his hand, Grandfather removed the cloth, revealing the gleaming green box. "This box represents my entire life's work—and Ratchet's as well. On the day he died, I vowed to find out whether there was any truth to his revolutionary theory about pure condensed light—no matter how long it took. And here I am, fifty years later, still working on it. Until tonight, all my conjectures about PCL and its role in explaining the evolution of stars were nothing but that: conjectures. Until I could actually identify its ingredients, I couldn't convince anyone it exists. I didn't have a ghost of a chance."

The mention of that word caused Kate to glance again over her shoulder at the hallway. Seeing no sign of anything unusual, she turned back to Grandfather.

"Have you tested the box yet?" she asked.

"Not yet," the old astronomer replied excitedly. "But the time is near."

"I still don't get it. How does making some substance that's found in stars allow you to travel faster than light?"

"Well," answered the inventor as he studied the humming box closely, "during my years of work on PCL I've learned enough about it to predict that it has some rather unusual properties. For example, it ought to melt anything frozen that touches it. But very recently—purely by accident—I discovered that it also has another property. An absolutely astonishing property."

Kate could feel his swelling enthusiasm and it stirred her own. "What property is that?"

Grandfather straightened his tall frame and looked squarely at her. "PCL has the ability to liberate the part of us most similar to pure light."

"You mean our souls?" asked Kate in wonderment.

"You could call it that," answered Grandfather. "People have given it many names in many languages across the ages. I call it our *heartlight*."

"But how, Grandfather? How does it work?"

"Only God knows the answer to that one, Kaitlyn. But if you keep asking—"

"Perhaps He'll give us a hint!" finished Kate, grinning. "But what does all this have to do with traveling faster than light?"

"Everything," replied Grandfather, taking her hands in his own. "When PCL is allowed to react with your inner light—with your heartlight—then you can travel anywhere in the universe, faster than light."

"I still don't understand how you could travel into outer space without a spaceship to take you there."

Grandfather's brow furrowed. "How can I explain it to you? Think of it like—like your imagination. All you need to do to go someplace in your imagination is to imagine it. Right? Then—presto!—you arrive there, faster than light. That's how heartlight works."

Kate leaned against the desk in utter amazement. Even if she didn't understand how heartlight worked, she finally understood why Grandfather had been working so hard.

"So this is why you wanted to study the wings of the morpho?" she asked quietly.

"Yes, Kaitlyn." His voice was almost a whisper. "It was the morpho who gave me the first clue that there is indeed a connection between the nature of light and the nature of the soul."

"You're saying that our souls and the stars and the wings of a butterfly are all somehow connected?"

"Yes," the old man agreed, nodding thoughtfully. "They are all part of God's great Pattern."

For a long moment, neither of them spoke. The only sounds were the humming of the green box, the vibrating of the beakers, and the continuous clattering of the machine in the corner of the lab.

At last Kate whispered: "If you're right about PCL and how it can free your heartlight to travel anywhere in the universe . . ."

"Where would I choose to go first?" finished Grandfather, his eyes alight. "Let me show you."

He led her across the room to a massive monitor screen next to his telescope. He switched it on, then began twirling one of the dials. Like a young child playing with his favorite toy, he typed some coordinates onto the keyboard.

With a flash, a highly magnified star appeared suddenly on the monitor. It radiated powerfully, and its shimmering red light seemed to reach right out of the screen and into the room itself. Behind Grandfather, the prisms on the table began to glow dimly red.

As he twisted more dials, the brightly colored gases of a great nebula surrounding the star came into view. They spiraled around it like a brilliant veil of incandescent clouds, finally fading into the deep darkness of space.

"It's beautiful," sighed Kate.

"That it is," replied Grandfather. "No other star is as beautiful as Trethoniel."

Pressing a button, he brought the swirling clouds into sharper focus, revealing several planets which orbited through the glowing gases of the star's system. One of them gleamed with a pearly white color. In the center of the spiraling veil, the great red star Trethoniel sat like an imperious queen upon her throne, unaging and untouchable.

"No other star in the sky radiates so strongly, Kaitlyn.

And here is the puzzle of puzzles: How can Trethoniel possibly stay so bright, without burning out completely and collapsing into a black hole? Scientists from all over the world—myself included—have failed to answer that important question. All I can say for sure is that it has something to do with its supply of PCL. Trethoniel is more advanced in manufacturing PCL than any star in the known universe. Meanwhile, it continues to flame, so powerfully that you can see it without a telescope even on full-moon nights."

Grandfather spun another dial, and the seething, scorching surface of the star completely filled the screen. Towers of superheated gases danced thousands of miles out into space. "On our world I am believed to know much," he said softly. "But one glimpse of this star reminds me how little, how very little, I truly understand. There is so much to learn about the Pattern."

He turned to the girl standing beside him. Her face, like his own, had been touched with a new and lovely light.

"Someday, Kaitlyn, if I'm right, people will explore Trethoniel and learn some of its secrets." He touched her braid gently. "Maybe you and I will be the very first to go."

"Me?" Kate shook her head. "Not a chance! I'm no explorer and I'm certainly no scientist! You'd be a lot better off going by yourself."

"What if I asked you to join me?" questioned Grandfather playfully.

"I guess I'd have to think about it," Kate replied with a grin. "But I'd rather you just sent me a postcard."

Her gaze returned to the image on the screen. "Trethoniel is full of mysteries, isn't it?"

"Right you are," agreed the old astronomer. "As Einstein said, *mystery is the essence of beauty*. No one can explain how Trethoniel could swell up like a giant red balloon—expanding to a thousand times its former size—then resist collapsing into a bottomless black hole. Traditional physics says that should have happened long ago. But Trethoniel has done exactly the opposite! Against every law of physics, it's grown steadily brighter, actually gaining luminosity with time. Its curve of binding energy is beyond anything we've ever known."

Grandfather studied the image on the screen. "When I first started observing you, Great Star, I watched you ceaselessly, like a vulture circling over some near-dead prey. Then, with time, I came to respect you more and more. I came to admire your beauty, your power, your desire to live."

"I'm glad Trethoniel is alive, too," said Kate quietly. "Somehow it makes me feel . . . well, hopeful."

"Yes," nodded Grandfather. He glanced at his own wrinkled hands, then turned back to the screen. "At least somewhere in the universe, mortality and death have been held at bay, if not entirely beaten." With a sigh, he continued: "One of the reasons Trethoniel is so intriguing is that it shares some extraordinary similarities with the Sun. Both stars are nearly the same age, probably condensed out of the same original cloud of swirling gases. And, before Trethoniel suddenly expanded and turned upside down all the laws of physics, it was a typical yellow star, just like the Sun."

At that moment, something new on the monitor screen caught Kate's eye.

"What's that dark place on Trethoniel, Grandfather?"

she asked, feeling strangely uneasy. "I don't think it was there just a few seconds ago."

Grandfather dismissed her question with a wave of his hand. "Probably just a storm on the surface or a simple refraction error, that's all. Nothing to worry about." He smiled. "By the way, how are you feeling? I mean, after your encounter with our friendly local ghosts?"

Kate shivered slightly. "They didn't feel so friendly to me. I'd forgotten about them, so I guess I'm fine now. Except . . . I just can't shake this feeling."

"What feeling?"

"I can't quite explain it. It's a feeling that something . . . something just isn't right around here."

Grandfather gave her a gentle squeeze. "It's probably just an aftereffect from your fright. Perhaps you—"

Buzzzzzz.

Kate jumped. "What's that noise?"

"It's the timer on the astro-vivometer," declared Grandfather. "My new invention over there in the corner."

He walked over to the contraption, which was shaped like a large gray file cabinet bearing numerous dials and switches on its face. "It can measure the level of PCL in any star, so I can assess the star's health and longevity with great accuracy."

"What was that timer for?"

"Oh, I've been doing a test run to make sure it works properly. I set it to work on the Sun, since it's the easiest star to analyze from Earth. The buzzer says it's finished the computations."

With an effort, Grandfather stooped down to pick up a printout that had dropped from a slot in the astro-vivometer. Suddenly, his face went white, and he whispered: "My God!"

"Grandfather!" cried Kate, hurrying to his side. "What is it?"

The old man gave no answer. He continued to scrutinize the printout, trying to check some of the calculations in his head. His expression grew more grim with every passing second.

"It must be mistaken," he muttered. "It must be."

"What does it say?" pleaded Kate, seeing nothing but rows of meaningless numbers and symbols crowding the printout.

At last Grandfather raised his head. Deep concern lined his brow, and the light of his breakthrough had vanished from his eyes. He looked at Kate somberly.

"What does it say?"

"It says the Sun is in trouble, Kaitlyn. Serious trouble." His gaze fell to the machine, still clattering away ceaselessly. "There could be a problem with the astrovivometer itself . . ."

"But you don't think so, do you?"

The old man turned again to Kate, and for a long moment they held each other's gaze. "No."

"What kind of trouble, Grandfather? Please tell me. What's going to happen to the Sun?"

Shaking his head sadly, Grandfather replied: "I—I don't know how to explain it, Kaitlyn. It's so—so enormous . . ."

"This sounds as bad as nuclear war."

Grandfather grimaced. With a quivering finger, he pointed to various numbers on the printout. "You see, there's been no change in the Sun's temperature, chemistry, density, magnetism, or surface dynamics. Only one factor has changed—the most important one."

"You mean its PCL?"

"Yes. If these figures are right, its core supply of PCL has started dropping at a precipitous rate."

"What does it mean, Grandfather?"

He drew his hand slowly across his brow. "If—if nothing happens to reverse it . . . then . . ."

"What? What then?"

"The Sun will eventually lose so much PCL that it will reach a state of catastrophic energy imbalance." Grandfather seemed to choke on the words as he spoke them. "Without any warning, it will collapse violently, and then—oh, Kaitlyn! The Sun will go out *forever*."

Kate stepped backward in disbelief. "But—but—the Earth . . ."

The white head nodded despondently. "We're not talking about any ordinary star, Kaitlyn. We're talking about the Sun. The life-giving, beneficent Sun! What the Egyptians worshipped as Ra, the Greeks as Helios, the Romans as Sol; the star that inspired the great temples of the Aztecs, the ancient circle of Stonehenge, and so much more. This means no more dawns and no more sunsets; no more lilies or roses or chrysanthemums; no more kangaroos or chipmunks, sequoias or sunflowers." He seemed to be talking to himself. "Millions of species, developed over millions of years—all wiped out in a single instant."

"But how can that be?" She struggled to take all this in. "It felt just like normal outside today."

Grandfather sighed. "This isn't something you can see or feel. Only an astro-vivometer is sensitive enough to discern what's happening inside the Sun. And the only one of those in existence is telling us we're in grave danger."

Pressing a blue button on the side on the machine, Grandfather pulled another printout from the slot. Instead of being covered with equations, this one bore an image, much like a blurred photograph. Kate knew instantly that it was a picture of the Sun.

"I haven't had time to bring the imaging capability up to speed," said Grandfather. "But this is good enough to show you. Do you see the dark blotch in the lower hemisphere?"

"It looks like a huge sunspot."

"If only it were! That is a PCL void deep within the core of the Sun. And according to the figures, it's spreading like a deadly cancer. At this rate, the Sun has no more than a thousand years left to live."

"A thousand years!" Kate felt suddenly relieved. "That's a pretty long time, Grandfather."

"Not to a star. To a star it's virtually nothing. If its natural lifespan hadn't been disrupted, the Sun would have had several billion years left to live."

Kate frowned. "How can this be happening? Why does our star have to be the one that's stricken by this—this disease?"

"I don't know, I don't know. I suppose it's all part of the Pattern, Kaitlyn. There is no other answer."

"What kind of Pattern would let such a thing happen?" exclaimed Kate. "If God really has some sort of Pattern, why does He let things die at all? Why doesn't He stop the Sun from collapsing and destroying the Earth and everything on it?"

The great eyebrows lifted. "Your grandmother would say that living and dying are both part of the Pattern.

When something in the universe dies, she believed, something else is born." Grandfather looked at Kate's worried face and placed his arm around her shoulder. "And remember this: God has also given us the gift of free will, and that's part of the Pattern, too. Maybe— just maybe—humanity can use its free will to find some way to save the Sun from premature death. After all, we still have a thousand years to find a cure."

Kate drew in a deep breath. "I guess a thousand years, while it's not much time for a star, is really a pretty long time for humanity to figure something out. Do you think it's possible that your discovery of PCL could help?"

"Perhaps," answered Grandfather. His gaze wandered from the astro-vivometer to the wall monitor, still glowing red from the light of Trethoniel, and a mysterious gleam shone in his eye. "Perhaps."

Lowering his arm, he spoke reassuringly. "We're safe for now, Kaitlyn. The Sun will rise again tomorrow . . . in not very long, as a matter of fact. In any case, it's time for me to get back to work. And for you to go to bed."

"Bed!" cried Kate. "But—"

"You need your sleep," he declared firmly. "Especially if you're going to be helping me in the lab tomorrow."

"In the lab?" Kate nearly jumped out of her sneakers. "Really?"

"You heard me, Kaitlyn. I've discovered today how much I need your company."

Kate turned and squeezed him as hard as she could. "Oh, Grandfather!"

"Please! Please!" he protested. "I have too much to do to get a broken rib."

She released the hug. "Can I ask you a favor?"

"You can ask."

"Would you mind—"

"Coming upstairs with you?" finished Grandfather. "Not in the slightest. I want to make sure myself there aren't any ghosts roaming around your bedroom."

"Thanks," breathed Kate.

"I don't blame you. After all, you had quite a fright. I'll leave the lab door open tonight, so if you get scared at all you can come right down here and join me." Seeing the look of gratitude in her eyes, Grandfather added: "And I'll do one thing more. I'll join you in saying prayers."

As they walked down the hallway to the stairs, Kate cast an eye into the kitchen. It seemed the same as usual; the light burned strongly. She sighed in relief and started up the stairs. By the time Grandfather had joined her, she had already brushed her teeth and pulled on her pajamas.

Together, they knelt beside the bed. The half-moon's pearly light drifted through the high window, across the soft cotton quilt, and over their clasped hands.

"What prayer shall we choose?" she asked.

Grandfather thought for a moment. "Let's sing the Tallis Canon," he replied. "It's the perfect thing for times like this."

"I remember when you first taught it to me, the night we went camping in Montana and we thought we heard a grizzly bear."

"Which turned out to be your father snoring," he chuckled. "I'll never forget that."

"Neither will he."

Suddenly, Grandfather's face grew serious. "Kaitlyn,"

he said softly, "if, for some reason . . ." Then he stopped himself. "I want you to know how much I love you."

Kate looked at him uneasily.

"Why don't you start the Canon?"

For a long moment, Kate searched the old man's eyes—for what, she wasn't certain. Finally, she spoke quietly: "I love you, too, Grandfather. And I always will. Please remember that."

"I will, Kaitlyn. Now start us."

Kate lifted her eyes to the window, glowing in the moonlight. Then she began to sing:

> *All praise to thee my Lord this night,*
> *For all the blessings of thy light.*
> *Keep me, O keep me, King of Kings,*
> *Beneath thine own almighty wings.*

Grandfather's gravelly tones rose to accompany her voice like a bass fiddle. Three times they sang the Canon, and each time their voices swelled stronger, until the room was filled with their melody and with a peculiar kind of warmth both beyond feeling yet fully tangible. As they finally fell silent, Kate could still hear the words *almighty wings* hovering in the air, like the fading echo of an iron bell.

At last Grandfather spoke again. "Time for sleep, Kaitlyn."

He kissed her gently on the forehead, then promptly turned and left the room.

Moonbeams fell across the quilt like lovely long arms, ready to carry Kate off to sleep. But sleep was still beyond her. In her chest rose a surge of excitement, and a touch of foreboding, about tomorrow.

In the darkness she felt she could hear anything, even the breath of a butterfly. The image of a lovely morpho, small and silent, came to her, beckoning her to float away on a gentle breeze of dreams.

Soon she was sound asleep.

GRANDFATHER re-entered the lab and moved directly to the astro-vivometer, not even pausing to inspect the green box still humming on his desk. He turned several dials, then pushed a button marked *Update*.

As he waited, he rubbed his chest, muttering: "So sore . . . perhaps she did break a rib after all."

Buzzzzzz.

Impatiently, he pulled the printout from the slot and began poring over it. "Oh, no!" he exclaimed, his face filled with horror. "This can't be right!"

Stuffing the printout into the pocket of his lab coat, he walked over to his desk and stiffly sat down. Reaching for his pocket calculator and clipboard, he somberly shook his head. "There must be some mistake. I'll have to recheck all the calculations. How can things have deteriorated so much in just half an hour? If PCL keeps vanishing at this rate, we'll have only *two or three* years before . . . before . . ."

As he labored feverishly, he didn't notice when the Sun's first rays started slowly to fill the sky. Songbirds, unaware of any peril, greeted the dawn with a chorus of celebratory chatter, and the room grew lighter by degrees. Fresh morning air began to mix with the slightly burned smell of the lab.

He raised his eyes from the clipboard and cocked his head hopefully at the astro-vivometer in the corner. "It's

time to check you again," he said aloud. "Perhaps it was
only a temporary fluctuation . . . perhaps the trend has
reversed. Then this will be a day of good tidings after
all."

The old man lifted himself wearily from the chair and
began to cross the room. "If only I had—"

Suddenly, he clutched his chest.

"No!" he gasped, staggering toward the door. "Not
now!"

Before he had taken another step, a new spasm of pain
shot through his chest. He buckled and collapsed on the
floor, knocking over a pile of papers as he fell.

3

the green box

KATE awoke to a wet tongue licking her face excitedly.

"Cumberland! Leave me alone!"

She rolled over, burying her head under the quilt.

The dog barked twice, leaped off the bed and padded to the top of the stairs. Then he turned, barked again, and waved his prominent tail like a red flag.

"What is it, Cumberland?" Kate lowered the quilt and stretched her arms. "What are you so worked up about?"

Cumberland barked again, then disappeared down the stairwell. As if taking no chances that Kate would change her mind, he sat at the bottom of the stairs and began to howl pitifully.

"All right, all right, I'm coming," she said as she rolled out of bed and quickly donned her jeans, sneakers, and a well-worn sweatshirt.

As she descended the stairs, Cumberland padded

swiftly into Grandfather's lab. Suddenly, Kate sensed trouble and she ran through the open door.

"Grandfather!" she screamed.

The old man was sprawled on the floor, surrounded by a mess of papers and notebooks. His skin was terribly pale and covered with perspiration. She rushed over to him, just as he began to stir slowly.

"Grandfather! What happened?"

"Ohhhhh," he moaned, rubbing his head and rolling over on his back. "I fell . . . But why now?" He looked up at Kate. "I'm fine, really. Just a bit dazed."

"I knew something bad was going to happen!" Kate's round eyes began to fill with tears. "I should have stayed right here with you instead of going to bed."

"Nonsense," said Grandfather as he forced himself to sit upright. "It feels like an elephant sat on my chest! I'll be fine, though. Give me a hand."

"Are you sure you should move?"

"Yes, yes. Just help me into the kitchen. A cup of strong tea is all I need. Then I must get back to work."

With Kate's assistance, he struggled to his feet. So wobbly was he that he had to lean against her with most of his weight to stay upright. Awkwardly, they negotiated the long hallway, stopping twice to rest against the bookshelves. Finally, they entered the kitchen, with Cumberland at their heels.

Kate helped him lower himself into the old rocker. Before he could object, she had covered him with Grandmother's picnic cloth and tucked it in around him.

"That will keep you warm," she said, breathing hard from exertion. She put some water in the tea kettle and placed it on the stove.

Cumberland seized the opportunity and started licking his master's face energetically.

"Down, boy!" Grandfather pushed him away, then looked at the dog severely. "Not now, Cumberland."

"You need to take better care of yourself," said Kate. "You gave me an awful scare! How did you fall, anyway?"

"Oh, I just fell, that's all. Must have tripped on something."

She looked at him piercingly. "That's not true, is it?"

The old man averted his eyes. "I suppose it could have been a minor heart attack. Nothing serious, though."

"Nothing serious!" Kate nearly lost hold of the kettle as she was filling the teapot. "A heart attack!"

"I've survived worse things," he grumbled. "I'm sturdier than you think."

"But a heart attack is serious," scolded Kate as she poured the brew into his favorite blue cup. "People *die* of heart attacks! You've got to slow down, Grandfather."

Wearily, he pushed some white hairs off his forehead. "I know you're worried about me, Kaitlyn. But I can't possibly die now. The Sun—"

"I don't care about the Sun! I care about you! I think we should call a doctor."

"No doctors are needed," said Grandfather testily. "All I need is that cup of tea that's growing cold as we speak."

"Here it is," said Kate as she handed him the cup. "Won't you please let me call a doctor?"

The old man's eyes flashed with determination. "The answer is No." He took a sip of tea, then studied her closely. "The Sun is in trouble, Kaitlyn," he said earnestly. "Much more trouble than I thought." He pulled the latest printout from his pocket and waved it before her face. "We could have only two or three years left! Maybe even less."

His words hit Kate like a splash of ice water. "I thought we had a thousand years!"

"So did I," answered Grandfather grimly. "But I was wrong! Now we have no time to spare. Here . . . help me get up."

"Are you sure you can do it?"

"Help me."

With a strong tug from Kate, the old astronomer rose shakily to his feet. Suddenly, his legs buckled and he fell back into the chair, knocking over the cup of tea.

"Drat!" he cursed, panting heavily. "Just when I most need my body to co-operate, it's failing me! Come, let's try again."

He reached a trembling arm toward Kate.

"No, Grandfather," she protested, tucking the picnic cloth around him again. "You should rest! Please stay in the chair! If you need something from the lab, I can get it for you."

Grandfather looked at her resignedly. "All right . . . Just until I'm a little more rested. Here's what I need you to do." He leaned forward in the rocker and whispered anxiously: "Go to the green box. Right next to—"

At that instant, Cumberland barked loudly and bounded out of the kitchen and down the hallway.

"What is it?" Kate asked.

Grandfather shook his head. "That's not like him."

From down in the lab, they heard the dog bark again frantically.

"I'll go check it out," said Kate as she ran down the long hallway, leaving Grandfather in the rocker.

As she entered the lab, she felt suddenly colder.

Just then she noticed the desk lamp was flickering and sputtering noisily. A blur of motion near the desk caught her eye.

"The ghost!" she screamed, as a frigid, formless cloud of white vapor began swirling around the desk—hovering, as if it were searching for something.

Then it began to coalesce around Grandfather's green box. Slowly, as Kate watched in horror, the green box lifted into the air, borne by the white vapors gathered around it.

"Stop!" she screamed, lunging after the green box. "You can't have it!"

The phantom cloud quivered, then suddenly blew her backward with the force of a hurricane—straight into the table laden with Grandfather's equipment.

Shattered glass and equipment flew in all directions. The table collapsed as she landed, sending tools and prisms skidding across the floor. The computer design terminal tottered precariously for an instant, then crashed to the floor with an explosion of glass. Brightly colored chemicals sprayed the walls and Kate's clothes.

"Stop!" she screamed, picking herself up again. Her head was sore and her wrist was bleeding from a flying shard of glass. All she could think of was Grandfather's life's work being destroyed.

The green box continued to float toward the door of the lab.

"No!" cried Kate hysterically. "That belongs to Grandfather!"

"Nnnoooo," came a voice like an iceberg cracking in two. It wasn't the kind of voice that Kate could hear with her ears; rather, it vibrated deep down inside of her

bones. *"Ittt bbellonnnggss tttoo mmmeeee."*

As suddenly as a bolt of lightning, Cumberland leaped at the green box, knocking it free from the ghost's grasp. The box skidded across the room and came to rest in the corner. Meanwhile, the retriever ran to Kate's side and began licking her wounded wrist.

For an instant, the ghost seemed to dissipate, like a cloud of poisonous gas dispersing with the breeze. Eyeing the box, Kate started to regain her feet.

Suddenly she saw one of Grandfather's largest lasers teetering and about to fall—directly on top of them.

"Look out!" she yelled, rolling to her side just as the heavy contraption came crashing to the floor.

Above the explosion of metal and glass, Cumberland's squeal of agony pierced the air.

"No!" cried Kate, crawling toward the helpless dog. "No!"

Cumberland lay motionless under the weight of the toppled machine. As Kate tried to lift the tangle of metal off his body, the air shivered with a laughter colder than death.

Like an evil wind, the ghost gathered up the green box, whisked through the door, and disappeared.

Kate could barely see for all the tears that filled her eyes. But she pulled and pried with all her strength. There was a sound of grinding metal when, at last, she lifted the heavy machine from Cumberland's body. Pushing against it with her shoulder, she shoved it aside.

Miraculously, the dog moved his prominent tail.

"Cumberland! You're alive!"

He whimpered pitifully, and Kate hugged his neck, burying her face in his flowing cloak. "You're alive!"

With an effort, Cumberland wriggled into a crouch

position. He whimpered again, then licked Kate's ear. Slowly, he rose to his feet and took a few halting steps.

"You're limping terribly." She tried to examine the dog's raised paw, but he drew it away as soon as she touched it. "And you may have broken a rib or something worse."

Kate forced herself to stand. Her head hurt where she had hit it, and she felt nauseous and dizzy. As she surveyed the room, her heart sank. Smashed equipment, splattered chemicals, broken glass, and scattered papers surrounded her. It looked as if someone had dropped a bomb in the middle of the lab.

At that moment, the full weight of the disaster descended. The box! The green box was gone!

"What's going on here?" Grandfather, looking exhausted, stepped into the lab. "It sounded like—oh, my God. This place is destroyed!"

Kate darted to the doorway and hugged him tightly. "The ghost," she blurted. "The ghost was here. In the lab!"

"Here? A ghost?" His voice was incredulous.

He kneeled to look her in the eye. "Are you all right, Kaitlyn? Are you hurt?"

"I'm fine," she said bravely, wiping the tears from her face. "Just a little dizzy. I hit my head, that's all. But he nearly killed Cumberland."

"What?"

The golden retriever barked loudly and limped over to them. Grandfather patted him and scratched behind his ear. "Cumberland, you old trooper! You're a match for any ghost." He turned again to Kate. "What did this ghost look like?"

"Like a ghost! Like a cloud or something . . . It wasn't

solid—sometimes it was practically invisible. We had a terrible fight. We tried to stop it from . . ." Tears began to well up again, but she fought them back. "Oh, Grandfather! It stole your green box."

"What?" The old man rose and scanned his desk, now surrounded by the wreckage of the lab. The spot where the box had once rested was vacant.

To Kate's astonishment, a slow smile spread across his face.

"But—but I don't understand," she objected. "It stole your box. Your special green box."

"Yes, I know," answered Grandfather, still looking at his desk and smiling broadly.

"Then what's so funny?"

He didn't respond.

"What's so funny?"

"It stole the wrong thing."

"Wrong thing!" exclaimed Kate. "I thought—"

"You thought the box was what I wanted. I know. That's because I hadn't finished telling you exactly what to bring me."

"But the green box—"

"Was needed for my research, that's all. Now that I've found the formula for PCL, it's no longer necessary. And I am quite sure it's not what our intruder was really after."

Stepping stiffly over broken glass and metal, Grandfather worked his way to the desk where the green box had once rested. Behind the minicomputer rested the rack of brightly colored beakers, still unbroken after the battle. From this rack, he pulled one simple beaker which held a half-inch deep pool of radiant green liquid.

"The best way to hide something special," Grandfather declared, "is to make it look as ordinary as possible." Holding the beaker high in the air, he announced: *"This* is what our intruder wanted, I'll warrant."

"What is it?" asked Kate, peering closely at the beaker. "What's so special about it?"

With considerable difficulty, Grandfather lifted his desk chair upright and sat down heavily. Then he turned to her and whispered in a tense voice: "There is something I didn't tell you last night, Kaitlyn. Something very important. I've not only identified all the ingredients of PCL—although that was difficult enough, believe me! No, I've done something far more difficult."

He glanced at the sparkling green fluid in the beaker and a smile flickered across his face. "I have actually *made* some PCL."

"Grandfather!"

"Yes." Grandfather straightened himself in the chair. "Last night I made the very first batch. No easy trick, without the intense heat and pressure of a star to help the chemistry along. But it worked. Now this beaker holds a small amount of the most precious substance found anywhere in the universe: pure condensed light."

"I can't believe it!" shouted Kate. "You fooled the ghost."

"Not for long, though. Once that intruder—whatever sort of being it really is—discovers it was fooled, my guess is it will come back."

Nervously, Kate glanced at the doorway. "Why would it want your PCL?"

Grandfather placed the beaker on the edge of the desk and frowned. "I don't know. It's useless to speculate. And right now we have more urgent matters to deal with. Can you make it over there to the astro-vivometer?

Push the button marked *Update,* then bring me the print-out so I can see it."

Deftly, Kate maneuvered across the wreckage-strewn floor to the astro-vivometer, which was still clattering noisily. She retrieved the printout and carried it back to Grandfather.

As she handed it to him, a look of such gravity filled his face that she at first thought he was having another heart attack.

"Heavens!" he muttered. "How can this be happening?"

"How bad is it?" asked Kate, almost afraid to hear the answer.

Grandfather looked at her with an ashen face. "Very bad. Very bad, indeed. The PCL drain is accelerating rapidly." He reached for her hand, and his voice was less than a whisper. "Unless something happens, the Sun will collapse in . . ."

Kate's heart froze in her chest. "In how long? Grandfather, how long?"

The old astronomer did not answer. "I must do something drastic," he whispered resolutely.

Fear flooded Kate's veins. "Grandfather, you're not well enough to do anything—let alone anything drastic. You could have another heart attack!"

"That's right," he said in a voice as hard as stone. "That's another reason I must act now. Too much is at stake, and we have almost no time left."

With that, he reached deep into one of his lab coat pockets. Carefully, he removed a small velvet box which resembled an ordinary ring case. As Kate looked on fearfully, he opened the box to reveal an unusual ring with a turquoise band. Instead of a jewel, however, upon the band was mounted a small transparent container crafted in the shape of a butterfly.

With a touch of his finger, Grandfather flipped open the top of the butterfly container on the ring. Then, holding the velvet box securely, he began to pour in the fluid. Concentrating intently, he watched it flow into the ring like sparkling syrup. Before he had emptied half of the beaker, the wings of the butterfly brimmed at full capacity, and the top snapped closed automatically. Waves of illumination flowed through the entire ring, like glowing coals at the base of a fire.

"What are you going to do with that?" demanded Kate, eyeing the velvet box and the mysterious object it held.

Grandfather's brow furrowed deeply. "I am going to do what I have labored many years to do, Kaitlyn. I had only hoped that the first time would be a moment of triumph, instead of desperation."

"But what are you going to do?"

The old astronomer looked deeply into her eyes. "I'm going to put on this ring. The instant I touch it, the pure condensed light inside it will set free the most alive part of myself, the part most akin to light."

"You mean you'll turn into light?"

"No, Kaitlyn. I will turn into *heartlight*. And then I can travel anywhere in the universe."

Kate shook her head in disbelief. "How can a ring do that?"

"It's made from a special conductive material, whose molecular structure is designed to bring the PCL in the ring into contact with the heartlight in my body. When that contact happens—well, just watch."

"But, Grandfather! You can't be sure it's going to work."

"I'm sure, Kaitlyn. I'm sure."

"Can't you at least wait until you're more rested?"

"There is no time left to wait," said Grandfather as he replaced the beaker on the desk.

"But where will you go? What can you do?"

"I will go to the one place in the universe that might provide me with enough information to find a cure—the place where more PCL is manufactured than anywhere else. I will go to—"

"Trethoniel!" Kate exclaimed.

"Yes! I don't know what I'm looking for, exactly. It may be some kind of substance, or process, that allows Trethoniel to make such enormous quantities of PCL. If somehow Trethoniel's secret could be applied to the Sun—"

"No, Grandfather, you can't! It's too dangerous. Your machine might be wrong . . . This could be a gigantic mistake. You'd be risking your life for nothing."

Grandfather shook his head. "It's no mistake. I am convinced."

"But you can't possibly go to Trethoniel and back in time."

The wild eyebrows climbed skyward. "Yes, I can. You see, Kaitlyn, time in interstellar travel is greatly expanded compared to time on Earth. It should take me only two or three minutes of our time to fly to Trethoniel, learn whatever I can about how it manufactures so much PCL, and return to help the Sun. Of course, it will feel like a lot more time, but by your watch I'll only be gone a few minutes. Besides, this ring holds only *four minutes' supply of PCL*—measured in Earth time, that is. So whether I like it or not, I can't be gone any longer than that."

"Only four minutes?" Kate struggled to comprehend.

"Yes. I haven't been able to figure out how to make PCL liberate heartlight for more than four minutes. There seems to be some sort of physical barrier halting the reaction at that point. I had hoped eventually to find some way to extend it, but without the green box, that's impossible now. And we have no more time for such experiments, anyway."

He looked thoughtfully at the radiant ring resting in the box. "I had even hoped that one day, Kaitlyn, you could travel with me—perhaps to the moon, or even to Mars . . ." His eyes glistened as he turned to her. "Maybe someday we'll still have that chance."

"No!" cried Kate, her own vision clouded with tears. A feeling of foreboding, stronger even than she had felt last night, swelled inside of her. "I don't want you to go! I have a feeling—a terrible feeling—that if you go you'll be in danger—worse danger than you can possibly imagine. Grandfather . . . please don't go. The risks are too great."

Grandfather touched her head gently. "There are risks, my child. I'm not going to say there aren't. There are still a few adjustments to the PCL I'd hoped to make before trying it out—one or two random elements I've not yet identified. Still, I think the ring should work. The risks are worth it, if there's any chance of saving the Sun. Can't you understand? All life on Earth is going to perish unless something changes soon. Everyone and everything on it will disappear forever."

Kate sighed miserably and looked at the floor.

"I am an old man, Kaitlyn. I'm going to die soon

enough as it is. You must understand. I've got to try."

She raised her head slowly. "Can I see the ring one more time?" she asked, her voice quivering.

The old man held out his hand, with the velvet box resting in his palm. The butterfly ring gleamed, radiant and mysterious.

Suddenly, she snatched the box from his hand.

"Kaitlyn!" shouted Grandfather, lurching after it.

"No!" Kate jumped out of reach. "I'm not going to let you do this to yourself," she declared. "You could be wrong about the way PCL works. You could even be wrong about the Sun. I won't let you do it, Grandfather."

A fire blazed in the old man's eyes, but he held his voice steady. "Now, Kaitlyn. Give me back the ring."

"I won't," she replied, darting behind the desk. Her mind was made up.

"Please," he begged, his hands shaking.

"No."

"Kaitlyn, please." He dropped his hands, and defeat was in his eyes. "All right," he whispered. "If I promise not to go anywhere until I've made absolutely certain that the astro-vivometer is right—that there's no chance at all of any mistakes—will you give me back the ring?"

Kate hesitated. "What if it takes you more time than the Sun has left to check the machine?"

The astronomer sighed in resignation. "That's a risk I'll just have to take. A risk we'll all have to take. But maybe—maybe you're right. Maybe there's some mistake after all."

"Do you really truly promise?" demanded Kate. "And not like your promises to finish working by a certain time! I want a *real* promise. The kind that makes you fry in agony and pain and horribleness if you break it."

Grandfather was beaten. Shoulders slumped, he whispered: "I promise."

Slowly, Kate walked over to his side. Closing the top of the velvet box, she placed it in his lab coat pocket. "I'm sorry, Grandfather, but I had to do it."

The old man didn't respond. He merely gazed despondently at the astro-vivometer in the corner. At length, he lifted his eyes toward her. "I feel so drained," he said wearily. "Since you've laid these chains on me, would you mind getting me some of that tea I never got to finish? It would give me the energy I need to walk over there and start working on the machine."

Feeling both triumphant and a little sad, Kate nodded. "One cup of tea with cream coming up."

She walked through the lab door and down to the kitchen, with Cumberland limping behind her. Making a whole pot of tea was as easy as a cup, so she prepared a full teapot of his favorite brew. Her thoughts drifted back to the ghost in the lab, and she shivered despite the heat of the stove. When the tea was ready, she put it on a tray and carried it carefully down the hallway.

As she turned into the lab, she suddenly let out a shriek. The teapot smashed on the floor.

Grandfather was gone.

"No!" she cried, running to the empty chair where he had been seated just a moment before. "He promised!"

Cumberland whimpered and sniffed the chair. Then he turned his soulful eyes toward Kate, as if to ask: "Where is he?"

Betrayed, Kate cursed the air and sat down dejectedly. "Grandfather!" she cried, hoping against hope that he would hear her and come back—from wherever he was.

There came no reply.

"I should never have trusted him," she moaned. "I never imagined he'd really break his promise . . . not that kind of promise."

Her eyes fell upon the beaker, still holding a small supply of the mysterious green fluid. She glared at it angrily, then turned toward the astro-vivometer. There it sat, clattering away relentlessly, oblivious to all the distress it had caused. It was as if nothing at all had changed, nothing at all had happened, as if Grandfather had just gone out for a little Sunday stroll around the moon, or maybe Mars.

At that instant, Kate had an idea.

Maybe Grandfather had another ring! He said he'd planned to take her with him—to the moon or to Mars. Maybe . . . maybe that was why he made so much extra PCL! Enough for *two* rings! If only she could find it— but where could it be?

Kate scanned the ruins of the lab. If she were Grandfather, where would she keep something so precious?

She thought hard. The telescope? No, he uses that too much . . . The freezer? No, that sometimes freezes shut and can't be opened for days. Where in this mess could anyone find anything? Maybe it's not even in the lab at all . . . There are so many places to hide things in this old house!

Then his words came drifting back to her: *The best way to hide something special is to make it look as ordinary as possible.* Was there a clue in there somewhere? But what could it mean? It isn't possible to make a butterfly ring look ordinary!

Kate shrugged her shoulders in discouragement. Then, by chance, her eyes fell on the old wooden bureau against the wall. The top-most of its slim drawers was slightly ajar.

"The butterfly bureau!" she exclaimed, darting over to it. Cumberland followed her eagerly.

As she drew open the drawer, a pale turquoise band flashed in the light.

Her heart leaped, and she started to reach for the ring. Then suddenly she drew back her hand.

What if it doesn't work? she asked herself. What if Grandfather didn't want to use this ring for a good reason? What if he didn't go to Trethoniel at all? She could never hope to find Trethoniel anyway. She could imagine it, but she had only seen it once. And even if she could find the star, she might never be able to locate Grandfather, or persuade him to come back home with her, let alone save him from whatever dangers awaited him.

Suddenly, the air in the lab became chilled, as if an arctic wind had blown through. The desk lamp started to sputter, and Cumberland growled deeply.

Kate froze.

"Wwwherrrre iisssss iittttt?" crackled an otherworldly voice from somewhere in the hallway.

Kate turned to the door, and again to the ring sitting in the drawer. Hurriedly, with trembling hands, she took the beaker, lifted the top, and poured in the precious green fluid. The ring snapped closed.

"Ggggiiivvve iittttt tttooo mmmeeeee."

She stared at the ring, but sheer fright kept her from putting it on. The ghost was back! The empty beaker fell from her hand onto the floor and splintered into pieces.

The lab grew quickly colder as a wisp of white vapor appeared in the doorway.

"*Iittttt iisssss mmmiinnnne.*"

Then everything became a blur of motion as the ghost sailed through the door, Cumberland leaped, and Kate reached for the ring.

4

the wings of morpheus

A heavy blue-green mist submerged Kate's vision and swirled about her like a cyclone, carrying her into a state of being she had never known before. There was no sound: only motion, motion, motion. Warm electric sensations coursed through and around her; she felt lighter, lighter than a bubble on a breeze.

Slowly, the blue-green color began to deepen, to thicken, until strange shapes began to form out of the wisps of mist surrounding her. On either side she could see the shimmering colors solidify into large, iridescent platforms. Could they be wings? Then she felt herself seated over a sleek black body with a round head directly in front of her. Simultaneously, two delicate antennae began to unfurl from the top of the head, quivering with new life.

"A morpho!" she cried, nearly falling off her perch. "I'm riding a morpho!"

As if in answer, the great flashing wings began beating in a mighty rhythm. Kate suddenly felt like a jockey astride a colossal racehorse. But there was no saddle to hold her steady and no bridle to guide her course.

"No!" she cried. "Stop moving! I'm going to fall off!"

But the powerful wings continued to beat. Kate clasped her arms tightly around the butterfly's neck, as the colored mist was swiftly replaced by thick white clouds.

In a dazzling burst of light the clouds parted and Kate could see the buildings of a town far below them. Her own town! There was the tower of the university chapel, and there was Grandfather's house. *I never did like heights*, she thought. A sudden wave of nausea passed through her, and she hugged ever more tightly the neck of her butterfly steed, pressing her face against its thick black fur. She shut her eyes, afraid to look down again.

Borne on brilliant blue-green wings, she rose swiftly through the clouds. Higher and higher she climbed. Eventually, she opened her eyes, just in time to see a group of snow geese emerging from a lumbering cumulus cloud ahead. She forced herself to glance downward at the hilly countryside fast receding in the distance. There was the Connecticut River . . . and were those the White Mountains in the distance? They seemed so small!

It dawned on Kate that she was climbing fast—at least ten thousand feet already—and yet her ears hadn't popped at all. This ride was far smoother than any airplane: She hadn't felt even the slightest jostling from air currents. Her eyes fell to the powerful pumping wings and she recalled the gentle touch on her arm of the morpho in the garden.

Without thinking, she glanced at her wrist. Curiously, the cut from the broken glass had disappeared; no sign of it remained. Even the small bloodstain on her sleeve had vanished. The butterfly ring sat securely on her finger, its miniature wings pulsing with luminescence.

Then Kate remembered the horrible sight of Cumberland trapped beneath the collapsed laser, and she shivered. *Poor Cumberland! I hope he's all right.*

Kate's grip loosened a notch, as she felt increasingly secure on the back of the smoothly soaring butterfly. At that moment, the snow geese passed beneath them, honking loudly. She watched in awe as the perfect V-formation sailed into another cloud.

More quickly than she would ever have guessed, the clouds themselves began to disappear. The surrounding atmosphere gradually grew thinner and darker. She leaned forward on the butterfly, straining to see, as the first small pinpoints of light began to emerge in the sky. Soon, the morpho wings began to glitter faintly with starlight.

Higher and higher they flew until finally, without warning, the butterfly's ascent slowed, then halted. Kate realized that she was floating freely, without the aid of any manmade machinery, at the outer edge of the atmosphere.

As she peered over the wide wings, Kate could see a deep blue planet, enrobed with white clouds, spinning far below them. It glowed like a sapphire, a delicate blue jewel both firm and fragile. From this perspective, Earth was more than the endless variety of settings and species that she had read about in books. It was a single, unified organism, a lovely island of life drifting in the silent sea of space. It was home.

She turned to face the familiar yellow star that had radiated sunlight for years numbered in the billions. It looked as constant as ever, ferociously hot, and powerful beyond anything she had ever known. It was difficult to the point of incredulity to imagine this fiery furnace ever going dark. Then again, she knew that before Copernicus it was difficult to the point of incredulity for anyone to imagine that the Sun, which swept across the sky each day for all to see, did not rotate around the Earth! Grandfather had once said that the Sun's energy output was the same as a hundred billion hydrogen bombs exploding every second; that it had delivered a hundred trillion kilowatt-hours of energy constantly to the Earth for several billion years. Could such fantastic power really be on the verge of dying? If so, how could Grandfather— one tiny human—possibly do anything to stop it? What if Trethoniel didn't show Grandfather the cure? What if she couldn't find him at all?

"Your questions are many and difficult, Kate," said a strange voice.

She looked frantically behind, above, and below the butterfly to find the source of the deep, melodic voice.

"And the answers may be as elusive as I seem, or as near as I am," spoke the voice again.

It was the butterfly itself!

"How do you know my name?" she cried, both amazed and afraid. She grasped the butterfly's neck more tightly. "How did you know what I was thinking?"

"You do ask many questions, Kate." The butterfly laughed, and it reminded Kate of a rolling wave booming on the ocean shore.

"How do you know my name?" she repeated.

"Because your ring, which has freed your heartlight,

has also brought me to life. I know more about you than you realize."

"Do you have a name yourself?"

"I am Morpheus," the butterfly declared. "My brother, Orpheus, is carrying your grandfather."

"Really?" Kate exclaimed, so excited she nearly lost her balance for an instant. "Your brother? Then you must know where Grandfather's gone!"

"I am afraid not," answered the butterfly. "Orpheus and I were created from the same materials on the same day in the laboratory—but I have no way of knowing where he may have flown. They could have gone anywhere in the universe."

With that, Morpheus turned his head sideways so that one of his two great green eyes, honeycombed with hundreds of facets, gleamed at her. For a moment, she gazed into the eye, captivated by its prisms within prisms within prisms.

"I never would have— " she began, then suddenly stopped herself. "I'm speaking without moving my mouth!"

"Quite right," replied Morpheus, with only a slight quivering of his antennae. "Now that you are made of heartlight, you no longer need your former voice. You can communicate with your thoughts alone, at least over short distances."

"This is a lot to get used to," replied Kate in disbelief. "Here I am floating on the back of a giant butterfly, miles above the Earth, and speaking telepathically. It's not possible!"

The long antennae waved in response. "So it seems to you, Kate, only because you have not experienced it before. There are wonders even more amazing on your home planet that you fully believe, simply because they are familiar to you."

"Like what?"

Morpheus slowly blinked his great green eyes. "Like the transformation of a wingless, earthbound caterpillar into a magnificent butterfly. Who would believe that such a thing could happen if it were not common knowledge? Who would predict that such an unimposing creature could construct a cocoon, exchange its worm-like body for another one of dazzling design, and fly off into the forest without a second thought?"

"I know that's amazing," said Kate, shaking her head, "but this is still too much to believe."

"More so than the tadpole who somehow becomes a frog? More so than the trees who manufacture food from beams of light? More so than the flowering spring, which follows the frozen winter? More so than the human child, once smaller than the smallest speck of dust, who comes to learn language, make tools, and bring forth a child of its own?"

"This is still more than I can handle," Kate replied. "How a simple ring could—" She halted, gazing at the butterfly ring on her finger.

"Something's wrong!" she cried. "It's damaged!" Indeed, the rim of the ring's left wing was roughly tattered, as if it had been eaten away by a powerful acid.

"Nothing is wrong," answered Morpheus calmly. "Your ring has begun to deteriorate, that's all."

"Deteriorate?" Kate clasped the butterfly's neck firmly. "What do you mean by that?" Then she remembered: Four minutes . . . that's what Grandfather said was the limit . . .

"The process of deterioration began the instant you

put on the ring, and it will continue until the ring has disappeared completely."

Kate stiffened. "You mean I can tell how much PCL is left by watching it, like the fuel gauge in a car?"

Morpheus waved his antennae in assent. "Except with this kind of car, running out of fuel would be fatal."

Gracefully, the butterfly spun his body around so that, instead of facing Earth, they were facing a dark sector of space. Dark, but for one pinpoint of reddish light that sparkled like a distant ruby.

"Is that where we're going?" asked Kate. "It looks so far away."

"Is it your desire to go to the star Trethoniel?"

"My only desire is to find Grandfather!" she exclaimed. "To make sure he's safe and to bring him home again. I have this dreadful feeling that somehow he's in much more danger than he realizes—from what, I don't know. If finding him means we have to go all the way to Trethoniel, then I guess that's what we'll have to do."

"I don't know where Orpheus has borne him, Kate, although my inner sense tells me it is someplace very distant. All I know are the instructions your grandfather programmed into the ring. You see, like you, this is my very first journey. But I can tell you this: Trethoniel is much farther away than it appears, and the journey there and back could be much more dangerous than you realize. I don't know whether your ring will last long enough to do all that."

Kate looked anxiously at the distant red star. "We have four minutes of Earth time."

The butterfly cocked his head pensively. "Four minutes of Earth time is not a great deal."

His repetition of those words struck Kate, to her own

surprise, as vaguely comforting. After all, how much could go wrong in only four minutes? Even in the expanded time of interstellar travel, four minutes didn't feel like very long. The real risk was that it wouldn't be enough time to find Grandfather, and she would be forced to return to Earth empty-handed.

"You must remember one cardinal rule," declared the great butterfly in a tone of voice that suddenly reminded Kate of her fears. "Never, but never, remove your ring."

She shuddered. "What would happen if I did?"

Morpheus studied her gravely. "If you should take off your ring, even for an instant, you would immediately revert to your normal human form. And in the realms where we are traveling—that means certain death. You could be vaporized by the fires of a star, suffocated by some poisonous atmosphere, or instantly frozen—but your ultimate fate would be the same."

"All right, all right!" exclaimed Kate. "I've got the message. I won't take off my ring."

"No matter what," emphasized Morpheus.

"No matter what."

"The only environment where you might have any chance at all to survive would be a planet with an atmosphere much like Earth's—and I don't have to tell you how unlikely that is."

Kate twisted the ring on her finger, making sure it was attached securely, and surveyed the endless darkness of space extending in all directions. "What if I fall off your back? The ring won't stop that from happening, will it?"

"It should," replied Morpheus. "I am the product of your heartlight reacting with the pure condensed light of the ring, and I am part of you now. As long as you're wearing the ring, I will remain tied to your heartlight. I will hear your every thought, sometimes even before you do. My guess is there's only one way you could leave my back, Kate: If you choose to."

"Fat chance of that happening," she replied, nervously biting her lip. It felt the same as her old lip, even if it were only made of whatever Morpheus said it was made of. "But won't we get burned by the heat of the star? We'll be going awfully close to it, won't we?"

"No, we won't get burned. You're now made of heartlight—and I'm made of pure light. You have no skin to be burned, and no eyes to be blinded by the brightness of Trethoniel."

"But I can still see you," objected Kate. "How can I see you if I don't have any eyes?"

"The same way you see in your imagination."

Kate turned to face the blue planet beneath them, silently spinning in space. She could see the thin, wispy edge of what must be Cape Cod, protruding from the body of North America like the prow of an ancient ship. So many shades of blue were there, they could not be counted; the whole planet gleamed with a luster more luminous than dawn's first light. Then, with a start, Kate realized how perfectly *round* is the Earth: Indeed, it felt as though she had never before understood the true meaning of the word. That very roundness seemed to emphasize the planet's vulnerability. Like a delicate bubble, its sweeping blue curves caressing the sea of outer space, the fragile Earth floated—helpless, lovely, and alone.

"I can feel pain in my imagination, too," said Kate quietly.

"Yes," answered Morpheus with a stirring of his

wings. "You can feel anything you could feel with a
body—and probably a few things more. You can feel
warm or cold; you can laugh or cry. The only difference
is that you lack a physical body that would be destroyed
by the elements and forces of space travel. You will even
continue breathing—although it's not air you will
breathe, but light from the stars around us. You are in
some ways physical, and in some ways metaphysical.
You are part light, and part beyond light. You are *heartlight*."

Kate gazed thoughtfully at the iridescent wings. "Do
you think there could be something out there—some
kind of force or something—that's dangerous to heartlight?"

"I don't know," replied Morpheus gravely. "There is
much that I don't know. That's why you must be very
sure you really want to travel all the way to Trethoniel."

For a few moments they drifted in silence at the edge
of outer space. No snow geese honked; no winds whistled. Kate felt all alone, poised at the boundary between
the known and the unknown.

At last, she spoke again. "I want to try, Morpheus. I
want to find him."

Instantly, the butterfly's powerful wings exploded into
action. Faster they raced, much faster than before, until
soon they were nothing but a vaguely blue blur against
the stars.

Kate stole a glance to the rear; Earth was no longer
in sight. The Sun itself quickly receded into deep darkness. Now there was no turning back. She turned forward again to see hundreds of new stars moving swiftly
toward them. The great glowing arch of the Milky Way
slowly submerged into a sea of speckled light, and be-

fore her eyes, the sword of Orion compressed into a tight knot of stars.

The ride was amazingly smooth. But for the whirring of the wings and the passage of the starry vista, it seemed as though they weren't moving at all. Kate slightly relaxed her grip on Morpheus' neck. Hearing the hum of his wings, but unable to see them anymore, she wondered for an instant if they were still there. Instinctively, she started to stretch her hand toward one of the invisible wings.

"Don't," warned Morpheus. "My wings are moving faster than light and they could slice anything that touches them to ribbons. That includes you, Kate."

Embarrassed, she withdrew her hand. *None of my thoughts are private anymore. Not even the stupidest ones.*

Quickly, however, she forgot the incident as they raced past hundreds upon hundreds of stars. So swiftly did Morpheus carry her that almost as soon as a star drew near, it had vanished behind them. It was like riding a rocket headlong into an endless meteor shower. Throughout, Kate kept her eye on one glowing red star in the deep distance.

"How many stars can there be?" she mused. "Is there any end to them?"

Morpheus gave no answer except to continue beating his powerful wings.

Suddenly, Kate was aware of a delicate, distant sound that seemed to permeate the silence of space.

"Morpheus! What's that?"

The antennae quivered uncertainly, as the wavering sound grew stronger. As they sailed swiftly into the sea of stars, Kate strained to hear. It was very difficult to catch more than a few faraway wisps of the slow, low, flowing tones.

Gradually, the swelling sound grew more and more resonant. The beautiful tones seemed to dance through the empty corridors of space, like something that was half music and half starlight. Celebration and peace moved through the melody; Kate had never heard anything so lovely. It felt closer and closer, and seemed to surround them, like the beating of some celestial heart.

A special phrase of Grandfather's popped into Kate's memory: *mysterium tremendum et fascinans*. She recalled the day he had discovered it in a medieval prayer and how happily he had shared it with her, saying it should be reserved only for rare moments of wonderment. *O great and wondrous mystery.*

She listened, eyes closed, for a timeless moment. Then she remembered another phrase, one from a poem by Wordsworth. Fortunately, she had read the poem in one of Grandfather's books, rather than at school, or it never would have lodged in her memory. As Wordsworth had entered a beautiful valley in Wales, he had found himself, as he put it, *disturbed with joy*. How, Kate had then wondered, could joy also be disturbing? It seemed an impossible contradiction. Now, for the first time, she felt a glimmer of understanding. But why did this strange music seem to bring those words to life?

Her thoughts turned to the stars whizzing past her: so many of them, and so beautiful! Could they be the source of the music? She recalled how Grandfather had once likened the story of a star's life to a great biography of Gandhi, Joan of Arc, or Abraham Lincoln: a compelling tale of birth, struggle, triumph, and violent death. He had said that every star eventually reaches a point where the age-old balance between its own gravity, which pulls inward, and its radiant energy, which pushes outward, will fall apart. If it's a normal star, like the Sun, it will suddenly shudder and compress down to the size of a moon. But if it's unusually massive, it could expand and expand like a luminous red balloon until— at last—it will burst and collapse so fast and so far that it will *disappear completely*, leaving nothing behind but a black hole.

Kate looked at the radiant glow of Trethoniel, still distant but drawing ever nearer, and she shuddered at the thought of any star, not just the Sun, dying in a final spasm that swallowed up all its energy and light forever. How wrong that such beauty should be doomed to disappear forever down some cosmic drain! Grandfather had once said that the gravity of a black hole is the strongest physical force in the universe—so strong that even light cannot escape. Did that mean that the heartlight of the living star is also trapped, without escape? Could it be lost forever to the universe?

"No, Kate." Morpheus did not wish to leave such a question unanswered. As the strange music washed over them, growing stronger by the second, he explained: "Energy can't be lost completely from the universe. It may be transformed into matter, and back again into energy, but it never totally vanishes. If an electron and a positron collide, they may annihilate each other, but they will still leave behind two photons—brand new particles—with exactly the same energy as before. And what is true at the tiniest level of the universe must also be true for a star. Even a star as big as Trethoniel."

"So the energy of a star that dies might show up somewhere else? In some new form?"

"Perhaps," answered Morpheus, his pulsing wings glistening with starlight. "Your physical body was made of material once manufactured inside of a star. So who can tell? Perhaps some of the energy of a dying star finds its way into the heart of a young girl on a distant planet."

"But what if the whole star gets sucked into a black hole?" demanded Kate, still distraught. "Nothing can get out of there—no light, no heartlight, no anything! Could all that life just vanish?"

Morpheus waved his long antennae gracefully, as if to comfort the hazel-eyed girl seated on his back. "Nothing totally vanishes, Kate. Life doesn't disappear forever. It only evolves."

". . . as part of the Pattern that Grandfather always talks about," Kate heard herself thinking. But she wasn't comforted. The haunting music now seemed more disturbing than joyful.

Suddenly, Kate realized that the great glowing mass of Trethoniel was upon them. Imperceptibly, Morpheus slowed the beating of his wings. Like a flower slowly unfurling, the swirling nebula surrounding the star opened into the spiraling veil she had seen on Grandfather's monitor. There, in the center, sat the magnificent star itself, encircled by a necklace of gleaming planets.

"Trethoniel!" cried Kate. "Is that where the music is coming from?"

"*Mysterium tremendum et fascinans,*" said Morpheus in answer.

Soon the great wings ceased beating entirely, and the travelers coasted in open space, illuminated by the shimmering light of Trethoniel and caressed by its music. At once, Kate understood that Trethoniel was not only a star, but also an entire system of planets, moons, and clouds of incandescent gases—as well as the spiraling nebula that wrapped around them all. How many times larger than the Sun's own solar system this star's realm must be, she could only guess. She looked in wonder at the luminous circles of light at the outermost edge of the nebula, sparkling like spherical rainbows decked with dew. The entire system seemed to whirl around itself like a dog that had chased its own tail since time began, and would continue to chase it as long as time lasted.

Then, abruptly, the music of Trethoniel faded away into silence.

"Where did it go?" cried Kate. She found herself clutching Morpheus' neck. "It was so beautiful! Why did it stop?"

"I don't know," answered Morpheus, sounding worried.

Kate shook her head. "And how—how will we ever find Grandfather in there? Trethoniel's system looks as big as a galaxy! He could be on any one of those planets—I see three or four at least—or somewhere on the other side where we can't see him, or even inside the star itself!"

"Or," added Morpheus grimly, "he could be in none of those places."

Kate's eyes fell from the radiant star to the butterfly ring upon her hand. She caught her breath. A large slice of the left wing was already gone!

Before she could even think the command, Morpheus beat his great wings again. Together, they sailed into the realm of Trethoniel.

5

the darkness

As if called by an inaudible voice, the great butterfly began beating his wings in a graceful rhythm. Steadily he carried Kate into the open arms of Trethoniel's spiraling nebula. As they entered the shimmering, shifting layers of light, Morpheus began to glide. With great swoops from side to side, they sailed deeper into the star's system, and nearer to the great red star itself.

Kate saw hundreds of objects, large and small, circling the star. In addition to the ones she had expected—planets, moons, asteroids—many strange and lovely formations danced around the star in stately orbit. Some seemingly solid forms were not solid at all when they were seen up close. Some were branching and bent like delicate ferns; others were pinnacles of clouds, whirling and swirling; still others looked like complex geometric crystals. She noticed one formation that resembled a gigantic snowflake, as large as a house. It sparkled like a great jewel as it slowly twirled in space. She wished Grandfather could see this; she could imagine the light of discovery in his eyes. Or had he, perhaps, already seen it?

Morpheus banked to the right to avoid a tangle of holohedral crystals that seemed to be swimming in tight formation, like a school of minnows. As the red light of Trethoniel glistened upon them, Kate wondered if there could be new forms of life here, life totally unlike anything on Earth. She knew how Grandfather would answer her question: *Only God knows the answer to that one, Kaitlyn. But if you keep asking . . .*

"Look there," said Morpheus, his antennae pointing to a creamy white globe emerging from a billowing mass of colored clouds in the distance. "It's Trethoniel's most remote planet."

"It looks like a big snowball," observed Kate. "I had no idea a planet could be so white."

She checked the butterfly ring. Nearly half of the ornament's left wing had disappeared, as had part of the left antenna. How fleeting would be her glimpse of Trethoniel!

As she gazed over Morpheus' broad wings and looked about herself, Kate's thoughts drifted momentarily from her search for Grandfather and the plight of the Sun. She was sailing inside a sanctuary, a slice of the universe all but unknown to earthbound observers. She knew that many great scientists (including the members of the Royal Society) would kill for the chance to see all this. How ironic that such an experience should be wasted on a girl who couldn't even stand science class.

"Wasted is a strong word," admonished Morpheus, as he banked to avoid an orbiting asteroid. "Maybe there is some aspect of Trethoniel that you can appreciate better than anyone else."

Kate furrowed her brow. "But I'm not a great scientist or a great anything!"

"That is true," answered Morpheus with a wave of his antennae. "You are just plain Kate. One day, perhaps, your great qualities will rise above your great insecurities."

"How can you say that?" she demanded. "You barely know me! You don't have any idea what a dunce I can be."

"I know you better than you realize." Morpheus turned his head and observed his passenger closely. "You, Kate, could change the course of the stars."

"Me?" Her gaze fell. "I'd be lucky to change the course of an asteroid! I can't even get Grandfather to eat regular meals, for heaven's sake! How could I possibly make a difference to a star?"

The butterfly shook his antennae in discouragement. "I'm coming to the conclusion that it would be easier to make a difference to a whole galaxy of stars than to convince you you're anything special."

"Just help me find Grandfather," said Kate testily. "That's enough for me."

As the gleaming white planet disappeared into a collection of clouds, a new formation, shimmering in the stellar breeze, caught Kate's attention. It resembled a kind of curtain, a curtain made of thousands of lavender-tinted icicles. She heard them tinkling gently as the winds passed through them, and the soothing sound helped her mood to pass as well. The lavender curtain glowed invitingly and billowed outward, as if in greeting, as they sailed by.

At that very moment, a vague and shadowy form was gathering itself deep within the bowels of the star. When seen from far away, it resembled a sinister cloud, darker than the foulest pollution ever to belch forth from any smokestack. So huge was its expanse that it could, in repose, obscure a large section of the star from view.

As it drew itself together, the dark form began to knot and tighten until, finally, it had condensed itself into a long, snakelike body—a body so dense that not even the powerful light of Trethoniel could pierce it, a body so black that only one name could describe it.

The Darkness. It was the ultimate void coalesced into a creature. Wherever The Darkness appeared, light withdrew; even as it slithered through space, it erased any light in its path.

The writhing shape of The Darkness lifted itself toward the unsuspecting travelers with frightening speed. Like a vast entrail of emptiness, it gleamed coldly in the starlight, a long and twisting mass with no discernible features save the single red eye, more a swirling electrical storm than an organ of sight, that glowed like an ember in its darkest place. As The Darkness streaked toward the travelers, waves of negative energy crackled around the red eye.

Suddenly, Morpheus felt a tingle of foreboding in his antennae. From the corner of his eye he could see the dark shape approaching rapidly. He swerved sharply and started to climb away from Trethoniel, beating his wings with all of his power.

"What's going on?" shouted Kate, caught by surprise. "Where are you—"

Her question was interrupted by the sight of the frightening form snaking toward them, leaving a trail of impenetrable blackness in its wake.

The Darkness coiled its fearsome tail and prepared to throw it like a mighty whip. With a searing explosion of negative energy, the tail lashed out, eliminating all the light in its path. It struck at precisely the spot where the travelers would have been but for Morpheus' quick change of direction. The whiplike crack of the tail sent powerful shock waves racing outward, demolishing the lavender curtain of crystals and several other formations floating nearby.

The shock waves crashed into Kate and Morpheus, sending them spinning through space. A hail of splintered crystals pounded them like a torrential rain.

"Help!" cried Kate when, for an instant, her legs lost their grip on the butterfly's back. She started to pitch to one side, as fear seized her. "I'm going to fall!"

"Hold on!" commanded Morpheus, wheeling around and dipping one wing like a rudder to regain his balance. "I won't let you fall!"

As the butterfly righted himself, Kate's panic ebbed only slightly. "I thought you said I couldn't fall off!" she exclaimed, grasping his neck tightly with her arms.

"This creature must be made of some kind of antilight!" cried Morpheus. "And it's strong enough to separate us."

"Then get us out of here!"

At that instant, the terrible tail struck again. With the weight of a massive moon, it smashed into a large asteroid floating just behind Morpheus. The asteroid exploded in a violent blast, throwing them into an uncontrolled spin. They tumbled through space like a leaf in a hurricane.

"Help!" screamed Kate in terror, as she started to slide off her perch. Her arms and hands clung desperately to Morpheus' broad neck, but the shock waves from the explosion knocked them upside down, then sideways, then upside down again.

She was slipping!

"Hold on!" cried Morpheus, working his wings desperately to halt their spin.

She tried to hold on to the morpho's neck with all her strength. Her heart pounded like a thundering drum. But the tighter she squeezed, the more she slipped to the side. Her fingers dug into the black fur covering the butterfly's body. With a final effort, she reached for one of Morpheus' slender legs . . .

Too late! She slid off the butterfly and fell headlong into the swirling mists.

She screamed—but the whirling winds screamed louder. Wildly she flailed her arms and legs.

Down, down, down she plummeted, like a sack of stones. So fast was she spinning that she could not see the floating crystals whizzing past her, nor even the great mass of Trethoniel itself coming closer and closer.

Nor could she see another shape, dark and sinewy, racing toward her. The red eye of The Darkness pulsed with desire as it drew nearer, approaching fast.

"Help me!" Kate shouted as she tumbled downward. "Morpheus!"

"I am coming!" the butterfly called, as he dove headlong to catch her. He rocketed past clouds and crystals like a shooting star. Then, to Morpheus' great horror, the serpentine form of The Darkness expanded at the end nearest to Kate, as if it were opening a cavernous mouth.

Morpheus beat his wings with all his might. Never before had he flown so fast! Now she was within his reach—even as the shadowy shape closed in from below.

With a crackling of negative energy, The Darkness closed itself about Kate, just a fraction of an instant before Morpheus shot past.

She was gone!

SUDDENLY, Kate felt herself completely embraced by darkness: damp, cold, and stifling. Her fall had been broken. But by what? At first the coldness reminded her of the ghost in Grandfather's lab—but this coldness was different: It was far more powerful, penetrating, and frightening. The ghost had been a chilling breeze, but this was more like an Arctic blast.

"Morpheus!" she cried, but the word could not pass beyond the heavy darkness surrounding her.

Gradually, Kate perceived something new. An eerie reddish glow began to flow toward her from all sides. And as it flowed it throbbed, like an aching wound. As irresistible as lava streaming down the cone of a volcano, the glow pressed upon her, trying to smother her.

She gasped. *I'm—I'm suffocating in here!*

The glow grew redder and deeper. It was everywhere. It was everything.

Kate writhed and kicked to get away from it. But there was no place to go. The glow gripped her even more tightly. Breathing with great difficulty, she put her hand on her chest, directly over her heart. It felt so weak! The beating seemed to be getting slower, fainter. Everything inside her felt squeezed, as if she were caught in the middle of a powerful vise.

She labored to breathe, but the red glow only grew stronger. It felt less like a color and more like a heavy woolen blanket, tightening around her, pressing the life out of her.

"Morpheus!" she cried. "Please help me!"

But Morpheus was too far away to hear, too far away to answer.

The deadly blanket grew heavier. Tighter. Everything around her was pulsing, squeezing, suspending Kate in its cold grasp. With shock, Kate realized that even her own breathing had taken on the same irresistible rhythm. She tried to move, but movement was increasingly difficult. She forced herself to inhale deeply—to break free from the powerful pulse. But its suffocating pressure was too strong. She broke into a spasm of coughing.

A bolt of fear shot through her. *I'm going to die! This thing is killing me!*

Then something inside of her stirred. Something deeper than fear. Something living, and breathing, and angry.

No, she protested weakly. *I don't want to die.*

The red glow pushed violently against her chest, and she coughed uncontrollably.

Tears streamed down her face as she struggled to regain a last measure of self-control. Instinctively, she moved her arm through the smothering cloud and touched her ring—the ring that Grandfather made, the ring that brought Morpheus to life. Somewhere deep within herself, a small candle was kindled.

With great difficulty, she drew in a shallow breath.

But it was her own breath, to her own rhythm. *No! You can't have me. I won't let you.*

Slowly, a new feeling started to swell inside her. Gradually, very gradually, her heart began to grow stronger, even as her breathing grew a little easier. The deadly vise seemed to loosen, one notch at a time, until she could feel some of her own strength returning. She kicked her legs angrily. Before long a new illumination seemed to fill her chest, and its warmth flowed through her every artery, like a cascade of liquid starlight.

Haltingly, unwillingly, the red glow began to recede. As the light within Kate expanded, The Darkness itself grew slightly thinner, so that she could suddenly see traces of Trethoniel's light through the shadowy folds around her.

She started to swim toward the light, pushing her way with all of her strength.

Then the air crackled vengefully, and the curtain of darkness started to descend again. A new wave of fear coursed through Kate.

"Morpheus!" she cried, before breaking into an uncontrollable spasm of coughing. "Help me! I—can't—breathe!"

MORPHEUS hurtled past The Darkness at a speed faster than lightning. What it was and where · it came from he did not know; all he knew was that it had swallowed Kate.

Cutting a wide arc through the swirling mists, he swung around to face the great writhing mass, whose red eye now blazed in triumph. Like an arrow shot from a mighty bow, Morpheus soared straight into battle.

The shadowy being condensed itself ever more tightly as it began to squeeze the life out of its prey. Suddenly Morpheus streaked past, almost brushing the red eye with his wing. The eye sizzled and crackled with rage and turned its attention to the riderless butterfly.

From the depths of space rose the whiplike tail, into which so much negativity had been squeezed that it could shatter any solid target or cancel out any light. Curling itself tightly, the tail lashed out at the butterfly.

Morpheus abruptly changed course and dove behind a floating blue crystal as big as an office building.

With a loud crackling, the deadly tail uncoiled, smashing directly into the crystal. Fragments flew in all directions, and the sound of the explosion reverberated throughout the realm of Trethoniel.

For an instant, Morpheus was unable to see any sign of The Darkness through the dust and remnants of the crystal. Still wincing from the shock of the impact, he could only discern the swath of impenetrable blackness left behind by the tail. No stars could be seen there, as if a slice of the sky had simply been erased. He knew that the evil energy of this dark creature could damage— if not destroy—Kate's heartlight.

Like a tiny hummingbird buzzing a giant serpent, Morpheus attacked the creature with all his fury. He dove and darted, spun and soared, occasionally piercing the edges of The Darkness but never inflicting any damage. Every few seconds the tail would coil like a deadly spring and strike, eliminating all the light in its path.

The brave butterfly tried to attack the electric red eye—which seemed to be the center of the creature's intelligence—but the violent swings of the tail kept him at bay. At one point, the dark mass near the eye suddenly grew lighter and more transparent. Through the swirling blackness, Morpheus glimpsed the form of a small girl.

"Kate!" he cried, and some of his flagging strength returned.

Instantly, Morpheus climbed higher until he was well out of range of the terrible tail. For a moment he circled and then, suddenly, he careened sharply and soared like a missile directly at the red eye.

The great tail held itself completely motionless. Whether out of confusion or design, The Darkness did nothing to remove itself from the path of its attacker.

Although his instinct warned him to beware of a trap, Morpheus did not alter his collision course with the motionless target. Faster than light itself he flew, bearing down on the sizzling center of the red eye.

Then, just as Morpheus approached, from the center of the eye there blew forth a terrible cloud of darkness so thick that no light could possibly penetrate. Trying desperately to avoid it, the butterfly veered upward.

Too late! A blanket of blackness descended over him. It was dark, as a black hole is dark, and cold, as death is cold.

"I can't see anything!" Morpheus cried, his eyes stinging with pain, as he fought to keep his bearings. Concentrated anti-light pressed against his wings with such force he could barely keep them moving.

At that very instant, the deadly tail coiled to strike at the tiny creature trapped within the black cloud.

Craaaack! A powerful explosion of negative energy and red lightning burst across the starscape as Morpheus forced his way out of the cloud and shot directly into the red eye.

The Darkness recoiled in pain. As it did so, it began

to dissipate. For an instant, Kate was visible again amidst the billowing folds of blackness.

Swiftly, Morpheus dove into the parting veil and careened to a halt beside her. "Grab on!" he cried.

She reached to him, even as The Darkness started to close again around them both.

"Grab on!"

As she wrapped her arms around Morpheus' neck, she felt something touch her leg from below. A thin and wiry tentacle, reaching out from the dark mass, began to tighten its grip around her leg.

"No!" Kate screamed. "Something's pulling me back!"

With all his strength, Morpheus tried to pull her upward. Slowly, he lifted her a small distance out of The Darkness, even as its folds gathered about them like enormous jaws. But the tentacle wrapped around her leg still more tightly and drew her down again.

"I'm losing my grip! Oh—Morpheus!" Kate's hands broke free of the butterfly and she was dragged downward.

Instantly, Morpheus wheeled around and dove beneath her. With a flash of his great wing, he sliced cleanly through the thin tentacle and caught Kate on his back. They shot straight out of The Darkness just as it came closing down behind them like a crashing wave.

"Thank you, thank you," she whispered, hugging the broad back of the butterfly as they whizzed away.

"We aren't free yet!" The wings of Morpheus whirred with all their power.

Sizzling with rage, the injured eye of The Darkness pulsed with pain. The tail lashed out, sweeping away the starlight in its path.

Morpheus swerved immediately before the tail whipped past. But its edge glanced against his wing—and the force of the blow sent him reeling. Kate was instantly thrown off his back and started tumbling through space, as the butterfly spun out of control.

"Help!" she screamed, suddenly robbed of her safety. "I'm falling!"

Downward she plummeted, drawn by the gravity of the white planet orbiting below. As she entered its thick atmosphere, she was pursued ever more closely by The Darkness, its red eye seething with desire. The writhing mass stretched toward her, groping, groping.

"No!" she screamed, seeing the shadowy shape approaching from above. "Noooo—"

Her scream was interrupted as she struck the side of a steeply sloping wall of snow and ice rising eighty thousand feet above the mountainous surface of the planet. Her free-fall now became a brutal terror as she rolled and bounced down the ridge of snow, like a tiny pebble thrown over a cliff.

Cruuuack!

A great burst of negative electricity filled the sky with red lightning as the terrible tail smashed against the ridge above her. Slamming into the mountain like a gigantic meteor, the tail broke loose an icy cornice and dislodged a tremendous wall of snow.

With a deafening roar, huge islands of white began to cascade down the mountainside, gathering crushing momentum as they fell. Thousands of tons tumbled together into a churning sea of snow, sending a billowing white cloud high into the atmosphere. The roar of the avalanche rocked the mountain to its roots.

As swiftly as it had started, the thunderous cascade

came to an end. The mass of snow settled, shifted once with a grinding lurch, then froze into place. But for the gentle wisps of white still hanging in the air, there was no sign of any violence, no sound but the steady sweep of wind across the virgin valleys. It looked as if this world of silent, snowy pinnacles had never been disturbed, by even so much as a footprint, for millions upon millions of years.

6

the cocoon

SUDDENLY, the world turned white.

All the sensations of the past few seconds whirled around in Kate's head: the first scrape of cold snow on her arms; the feeling of falling down a bottomless slide, bouncing and somersaulting with terrifying speed; the dark cracks that snaked swiftly across the slope; the wall of snow rising above her, pushing her ever faster until, like a breaking wave, it collapsed over her, tossing and tearing at her helpless form; and, throughout, the thunderous roar of the avalanche.

Now all was still. All except the thunder, which continued to drum in her ears. She shuddered at the memory of the dark form reaching to grab her—and that horrible eye, seething and sizzling like a whirlpool of red lightning.

She struggled to lower her hands, which had instinctively covered her face as the wave of snow crashed over her. But she could only move with great effort inside her tight cocoon. She wriggled and squirmed and finally succeeded in creating a small space around her head.

A feeling as cold as the snow surrounding her slowly seeped into her consciousness. *I'm trapped! I'll never find Grandfather now!*

Kate felt limp, tired, and helpless.

Then the image of Morpheus, battling gallantly to save her, came into her mind. Perhaps he could help her again! She concentrated her thoughts on the great flashing wings.

"I'm here!" she called. "Can you hear me?"

No answer penetrated the darkness. No movement. No sound.

She gathered her energy and continued to try. "Morpheus!" she called. "Morpheus . . . Can you hear me?"

Still no answer. Only a dull, distant feeling of pain and loss.

Maybe I can dig myself out! Then Morpheus can find me! She shivered, from more than the cold. The dark creature too would be waiting to find her.

With a sideways twist, she managed to free her shoulders slightly. A growing need to rest, to sleep, rose inside her, but she resisted it. Again she twisted, and again her tomb of snow loosened its grip a few degrees, but no more. The tips of her fingers began to ache with cold.

She paused, allowing her limbs to relax. Her heart was pounding, and it seemed somehow to be beating louder than it had since she had left Grandfather's lab. Perhaps this chamber of snow was magnifying the sound? A sudden flash of memory recalled the smothering red glow inside The Darkness, and she released a cry of pain.

Her heart pounded even louder, and she struggled to

regain her composure—and not to panic. *There's no red glow in here . . . only snow. Lots of snow. I can still dig myself out. It doesn't matter how long it takes. I'm made of heartlight. I can't freeze to death.*

She swallowed her fears and forced herself to think. First she must figure out which way is up. Otherwise she might dig in the wrong direction.

A wave of uncertainty washed over her. If only she could see . . .

Then an idea flashed in the darkness. *I don't need to see! All I need is gravity. That's it, gravity!*

Pleased with her own ingenuity, Kate hatched a plan. With considerable effort, she pushed away enough snow to create a large cavity around her head and chest. She placed one hand in front of her face and, with a hearty ptttew!, spit a stream of saliva into her palm. *Whichever way it rolls, I'll dig in the opposite direction.*

Slowly, she felt the liquid gather and begin to trickle . . . up her fingers, away from her palm. With satisfaction, she knew that the avalanche had left her upside down. Before she could dig herself out, she must turn around.

Then an icy tremor shook her to the core.

Her hand! What was happening to it?

With frightening swiftness, her hand grew stiff, like wood, and deeply chilled. She tried to squeeze it into a fist, but the base of her fingers had hardened so much that she couldn't bend them. In the darkness, she slid her other hand next to the afflicted one. As her fingertips reached out to touch the stiffened palm, they struck an icy, frozen surface, a surface that had lost its sense of touch.

I'm freezing! she realized, in shock and confusion.

She twisted violently, trying to draw her knees into her chest. They felt heavy and numb.

What was happening? How could this be . . . unless . . .

She reached in the darkness to touch her butterfly ring. Gone!

Tears, real tears, began to well up in Kate's eyes as she realized that somewhere in the vast mountain of snow squeezing her from all sides was her precious ring. What had Morpheus said would befall her if she ever lost it? *Certain death—vaporized by the fires of a star, suffocated by some poisonous atmosphere, or instantly frozen . . .*

Frozen! Is that how this quest was to end?

Remorse deeper than the snows of this frozen planet suddenly fell upon her. Grandfather will feel as if he killed her, blaming himself for everything. But she did it to herself! Why did she ever think she could find him in the first place? She should never have left the lab . . . She should have let that ghost take the ring! Then it might be the ghost who ended up getting buried alive on some faraway planet . . .

She tried to flex her legs and arms, if only to keep the circulation moving. A deep, dull sensation of heaviness was moving through every cell of her body. She shivered uncontrollably and her teeth began to chatter. Her entire body felt increasingly numb.

And cold, cold!

Kate's eyes felt heavy, and she let them fall closed for an instant. Sleep would feel so good, so peaceful . . . would save her energy for later . . . would give her the rest she deserved . . .

No! I must not sleep. That would be the easy way out.

It would be suicide. Maybe Morpheus is digging for me this very second.

She listened for any sounds at all. The only thing she could hear was the pounding of her heart, her true heart, inside her small body. The beating was still there, but slower, more subdued. She listened for a while to the rhythmic pulsing, which made her feel drowsy again. Her eyelids drooped heavily.

A strange sense of calm began to envelop her. Instead of alarm, she felt only weariness. Instead of anger, she felt only sorrow. How sad never to see Grandfather again, nor to run with Cumberland again, nor to sing favorite songs with Dad again. How sad never again to smell the aroma of Mom's bread baking in the kitchen, never again to see the great wings of Morpheus flash in the starlight, never again to hear the music of Trethoniel . . .

Suddenly her body shivered with a tremor of cold, and this reawakened her. *How can I fight off this sleep?* raced her thoughts. *It's getting harder and harder. I can't stay awake much longer.*

Then some words and music from a faraway time and place drifted back to her, echoing in her mind as they had once echoed in a tiny room on a distant planet:

> *All praise to thee my Lord this night,*
> *For all the blessings of thy light.*

Another spasm of chills shot through her. She mustered all of her remaining strength and forced herself to dig, using her throbbing hands as shovels. Slowly, she loosened enough of the snow to turn her body around, then started to work her way upward. And as she worked, Kate began to sing again, as loudly as she could.

Keep me, O keep me, King of Kings . . .

She pressed her numbing fingers against her unfeeling cheeks as her teeth chattered through the words *King of Kings*.

Beneath . . . thine own . . . almighty wings . . .

She continued to dig, handful by handful, stopping only to push her hands into her armpits for a touch of warmth. But the feeling had left them, and soon they felt no more alive than trowels made of metal. Wearily, she pressed on, digging, digging.

At one point, a clump of wet snow came loose and fell with a splat onto her face. She tried to brush it off, but she struck herself in the eye with her own frozen fingers. She shook her head angrily, trying to remove the snow that had mixed with her perspiration and tears. The pain in her arms was excruciating. She wanted to scream, not to sing!

She wasn't getting anywhere. After all this digging, she had moved only a few feet, if that. Who could tell how far she still had to go? This was hopeless!

She slapped her hand against the wall of snow, half expecting it to splinter into pieces. She was freezing! Her hands and feet had no feeling left. What would Grandfather do now? What would he tell her?

At once, she knew: *Perseverance, Kaitlyn . . . If there is any quality I wish for you, it's perseverance.*

A rush of longing filled her heart—longing for Grandfather, for his voice, for his arms around her. Just to hear him tell one of his stories . . . just to hear him laugh. Maybe he's in trouble, too. Maybe he needs help! Suddenly, Kate knew what she had to do, despite the pain.

She had to try.

With grim determination, she started again to dig. To dig and to sing.

> All praise to thee . . . my Lord this night,
> For all the blessings . . . of thy light.

With each phrase, she climbed a little higher, although she could not tell whether she was six feet or six hundred feet from the surface.

> Keep me, O keep me . . . King of Kings . . .

Like a relentless machine, she pressed ahead. Her hands, feet, and face were now completely numb; she couldn't even feel the touch of her own tongue on her lips. Her entire body felt heavier and heavier and she knew she had little strength left.

> Beneath thine own Almighty . . .

Without warning, she slipped backward, bouncing violently against the snow. She could not fall very far; the loose snow she had dug had filled up the cavern beneath her. But it felt as if she had lost all the ground she had gained. She landed with her leg twisted beneath her body. Yet the limb felt only a vague, dull pain: It too was beginning to turn into lifeless stone. Exhausted, she sank back against the snow, too weary to move.

Then, in a distant memory, she heard Grandfather's voice again. *Perseverance, Kaitlyn.*

She shook herself, determined at least to clamber back to the place from which she had fallen.

Desperately, she tried to concentrate. To dig. With a final effort, she swung her hand into the snow above her head.

In a dazzling blaze of light, her hand burst through the surface. Crisp, cold air flowed over her. Utterly exhausted, she mustered barely enough strength to climb out of the tunnel before collapsing, face down, on the snow. Her frosted braid lay across her back as stiff and straight as an arrow.

7

ariella

THE vast snowscape was as still as it was silent. But for the prominent plumes of snow blowing from the ridge of peaks encircling the valley, there was no movement at all.

Then, from out of the drifts appeared two figures, glistening with the same whiteness as the snow itself. One, shaped like a large hexagonal snow crystal, rolled across the crusted surface with ease, leaving no trace; the other, built like a lanky column of ice, moved more clumsily. They approached the helpless body sprawled upon the snow.

"There it is," said the hexagonal being, pointing to Kate with an outstretched arm. The delicate voice tinkled melodically, like a wind chime made of brass. "There is the creature who made the sounds."

"An ugly thing, isn't it?" observed the other being. "Just like the sounds."

"Don't be silly, Spike. Those sounds were beautiful. A little strange, but still beautiful."

"Nothing this ugly could do anything beautiful. Ariella, you're always imagining that things are better than they really are."

"Does that include you?" she retorted, surveying the columnar crystal with disdain. Then, focusing on Kate, Ariella opened wide her eyes—eyes that glistened with the same silvery sparkle as the other People of the Snow. She gently laid one of her six delicate arms on Kate's back and listened intently.

"I think it's still alive," said the young snow crystal at last. "Just barely."

"Forget it, Ariella!" Spike lifted himself to his full height of almost three feet and regarded his friend scornfully. "We don't have the slightest idea where this creature came from, or whether it's dangerous to Snow People. It definitely doesn't belong on this planet, with that sort of body. It probably carries some terrible disease that could contaminate us all!"

"I don't think so," replied Ariella, bending closer to Kate. "But I am sure of one thing: If we don't act quickly, it will certainly perish."

Spike shook his long face from side to side. "So let it perish! Why can't you Hexagonals just leave well enough alone? You're always trying to heal things, even when the world would be better off without your help. I suggest we forget about it and go back home."

Ariella gazed at Kate with her round, soulful eyes. "Any being that can sing so beautifully deserves to live."

"I suppose you know some kind of secret Nurse Crystal remedy that can bring this creature back to life," said Spike sarcastically. "Didn't your mother teach you one?"

Ariella glowered at him. "The Nurse Crystals brought you back . . . or have you forgotten that already?"

Spike shifted uncomfortably. "So they got lucky! So what?"

"They may have repaired your body, but they couldn't do much for your personality." Ariella turned again to Kate. "Now," she said quietly to herself, "what was that remedy for frozen tissue?"

She lifted Kate's lifeless hand, then closed her eyes in deep concentration.

"Give up, Ariella," urged her companion after several seconds had passed. "This creature is beyond hope."

Ariella continued to hold Kate's hand and sang softly to her. The gentle song, full of soothing tones, filled the silence of the snowy valley. Her crystalline face, set in the middle of her hexagonal body, glowed with a warmth that seemed radically out of place on this frozen planet. Outward the warmth poured, through the crystal's ornamented arms and into the girl's ashen body.

"Yes, yes," whispered Ariella, her eyes still closed. "Not too fast, now. The slower we go the less risk of damage. Take your time, take your time."

Slowly, imperceptibly, a touch of color returned to Kate's face. At length, she moved her fingers in Ariella's hand. Soon a ruddy tone returned to her skin. Then, with an effort, she opened her eyes.

She started at the sight of the strange creature bending over her. "Who are you?" she cried, trying to crawl away.

"You tell us first," replied Spike, peering down at her. "You tell us, then we'll tell you."

Two creatures! realized Kate. *All that work just to end up trapped by—*

"I am Ariella and I am your friend," declared the hexagonal snow crystal, her telepathic words cutting short Kate's thought. She cast a sidelong glance at Spike. "Don't mind him. He never learned any manners."

"And you never learned any common sense!" blustered Spike angrily. "You don't even know if this creature is good or evil!"

"I don't know if I'm good," answered Kate weakly. "But I don't think I'm evil."

Ariella's eyes glowed with humor. "That's a pretty good answer."

Spike pointed to Kate's leg. "If you're not evil, then what is *that?*"

Clinging fast to Kate's left ankle was the remains of the tentacle that had grasped her in The Darkness.

"Oh!" Kate jumped with fright, rolling into Spike. "Get it off! Get it off me!"

"You claim it's not part of you?" questioned Spike, as he regained his balance.

"Get it off!" shrieked Kate. She yanked at the tentacle, finally pulling it free with a crackle of negative energy, and hurled it hatefully against a drift.

Ariella cringed at the sight of the horrid appendage that had twisted itself into a twitching knot of blackness sizzling on the snow.

"So cold!" cried Kate as she put her hand under her armpit to warm it again. "That thing is ten times colder than even this frozen planet."

"You see?" Spike observed cynically. "She's not from this planet."

"No, I'm not!" Kate couldn't keep the tears from flooding her eyes. "I'm from someplace warm! I'm from Earth! I came here searching for Grandfather—and I've got to find him! Everything was fine until the dark thing attacked us and I fell off Morpheus' back and it tried to suffocate me and—"

Suddenly she felt dizzy and started to fall backward. As she collapsed on the snow, the chill from her hand deepened. Swiftly, like a cancer, the frozen feeling again began to spread throughout her body.

"I'm—I'm freezing!" she chattered, flapping her arms against herself.

"Of course," said Spike scornfully. "That's what you get for digging in the snow when you're not built for it. I'm built for it—and I never dig unless I'm forced to."

"Be quiet, Spike." Ariella looked at Kate sympathetically. "You moved too quickly, I'm afraid. Your body is still on the edge of iceness."

"I'm so c-cold!"

"You must relax."

"I can't relax! I'll freeze. Even my tears are freezing!"

Ariella closed her eyes in concentration. She began turning herself around and around on the snow, until she was twirling in place like a crystalline top. Faster and faster did she spin, so that soon she was no longer a flat hexagonal crystal but a glittering globe, whirling with a subdued silver radiance.

Shivering with cold, Kate watched as Ariella suddenly stepped out of the whirling globe. Instantly, it began to condense into a transparent veil of shimmering light.

Ariella reached for the silver veil and draped it over Kate like a large beach towel. She spread it over Kate's head, arms, and hands, taking special care to cover the hand which had torn the dark tentacle from her leg. Then she stretched the veil over Kate's legs and feet, sealing it at the edges with swift movements of her six long arms.

"How do you feel now?"

"C-cold," chattered Kate.

"Just wait," said Ariella, gently touching Kate's forehead with the tip of one of her arms.

To Kate's surprise, the crystal's touch was not icy and hard, but warm and mysteriously soft. Then she noticed that thousands of delicate white hairs covered Ariella's crystalline body. Her broad face had no mouth, since the People of the Snow could communicate telepathically, nor even an obvious top or bottom; its only features were the two round eyes that glowed like full moons.

Slowly, Kate could feel herself relaxing. "I feel—I feel a bit warmer," she said.

"Good. Just rest a moment so the cloak can do its work."

As Kate sat on the snow, the airy veil began to seep gradually into her body. As it did, her entire self grew warmer, from the inside out as well as from the outside in.

"This is better than a cup of hot chocolate," she joked.

Ariella's face wrinkled in concern. "A what? You're delirious. Just relax."

Kate smiled, and a new surge of warmth filled her body. "Hot chocolate. I'll explain it to you later."

By now the veil of silver light had soaked into her body so that it was completely invisible. Kate felt warm and protected, as if she were covered by an arctic suit of heavy down. Slowly, awkwardly, she rose to her feet.

"You have traveled a long way," said Ariella softly. "How would you like to come home with us?"

"Speak for yourself, you stupid Hex," muttered Spike, still keeping his distance.

"I am speaking for myself," glared Ariella. "You can stay out here forever, for all I care." She turned again to Kate. "By the way, what is your name?"

"Kate. Kate Prancer Gordon."

"And you say you're from somewhere called Earth? Is that a long way from here?"

"Not if you're made of heartlight."

"Of what?"

"Heartlight. I can't explain it. Something like imagination, but better." Kate hung her head. "Anyway, I'll never make that trip again, because I've lost my ring."

"Your what?"

"My ring."

"What is that?"

Kate hesitated. "It's like—like a bracelet, but instead of being for your arm, it's for your finger."

"And what is a finger?"

Kate waved her fingers and saw Ariella study them curiously.

The snow crystal's eyes reflected her puzzlement. "Why do you need little arms like that at the end of your arms? They could freeze so easily! And you say this thing called a ring brought you here?"

"Well, sort of. It's a special kind of ring that brings out your heartlight. So you can travel anywhere. It was Morpheus who really brought me here, but unless I'm wearing the ring I don't think he can find me again."

Ariella's face showed complete confusion. Meanwhile, Spike's face showed mostly disdain, although his eyes glinted with something more.

"Oh, well," said Ariella, erasing her doubts for the

moment. "Would you like to come home with me? My mother doesn't have any rings, I'm sure, but she does have some beautiful bracelets. And perhaps she will know some way to help you."

Kate nodded.

Ariella faced Spike squarely. Her silver eyes opened to their widest, as she declared: "You're welcome to come, too, but only if you start to show some manners."

"No, thanks," answered the columnar crystal. "I'd rather not be seen with an alien. And I'd like to do some more exploring. That's what we came out here to do today, until you decided to play Nurse Crystal."

Kate turned to Spike. "I know you don't like me, for some reason," she said. "But I still want to thank you for saving my life."

He merely grunted and looked away.

Lifting her eyes to the pinnacled ridge of peaks, Kate's gaze floated over them like a slow-flying hawk. She exhaled a puff of frosty white vapor. The air tasted fresh and clean, not unlike the mountain air of the Rockies or the Scottish highlands where she had hiked with Grandfather. Yet it was different: fuller, richer, and more humid. This air had weight where the air of earthly mountains had none.

She walked a few steps on the velvety blanket of snow. Despite her brush with death, she felt light and strong, almost glad to have a body again. Perhaps it was the fact, which she had no way of knowing, that this planet had only eighty-five percent of the gravitational pull of Earth; perhaps it was the richness of the mountain air, which flowed over her like a tumbling brook. She drew in another full breath, tasted its crystalline quality, then exhaled.

"This place is like Shangri-La."

"I don't know that place," replied Ariella, who was leaning against a small drift nearby. "But I do like the sound of the name."

Her voice lifted into a sparkling, musical laughter, the sweetest laughter Kate had ever heard. It sounded like the chiming of distant church bells.

Focusing on the snow crystal, Kate looked deeply into the eyes that resembled bottomless pools of light. "I owe you my life," she said quietly.

"You looked very peaceful there," replied Ariella. "But I felt you wanted to live some more."

"How could you tell?"

"That song you sang," answered the snow crystal. "It sounded so full of faith and love . . . like the music our star Trethoniel used to make."

"Used to make?"

"Before the Great Trouble began," replied Ariella, suddenly somber. Then, just as abruptly, she bubbled up with a playful thought: "How would you like to go sledding with me? It's the quickest way home, and the most fun, too."

"What do you mean by *the Great Trouble*?"

"I don't want to talk about it."

"But it might help—"

"Let's go sledding."

With those words, Ariella instantly cartwheeled to Kate's side, then slid herself like a large dinner plate under her feet. "Now, sit down," she commanded. "Then push! You're heavier than what I'm used to."

Awkwardly, Kate sat upon the crystalline creature. She grudgingly gave a push against the cold snow, then grabbed two of Ariella's outstretched arms for balance.

Suddenly she realized that they were starting to slide down the same slope that had nearly buried her alive not long ago. "Not too fast!" she yelled as wet snow began to spray in her face.

"Don't worry!" called Ariella. "I never get caught in avalanches, except for fun."

"Fun!" Kate almost fell over sideways.

"Don't worry!" called Ariella. "I know all the safe routes."

They gathered speed like a bobsled on its run. Ariella did indeed seem to know her way as she glided along ice walls, careened away from snowy overhangs, and slid past towering outcroppings of rock.

As they sailed down the slope, Kate noticed row after row of rainbows in the spraying snow. Towering above them were the glistening ridges of mountains more than twice as high as any on Earth.

"Hold on!"

At that instant, she saw an enormous wall of ice looming directly ahead. They were heading straight for it, at terrifying speed, with no time to make any turns. Kate gripped Ariella's arms tightly and closed her eyes.

Without warning, they dropped into a hole in the snow. Darkness instantly surrounded them, as they slid down a chute of ice. After taking several rapid turns, the tunnel began to angle gradually upward, and Kate could see a hole of light fast approaching.

Like the cork of a champagne bottle, they shot out of the tunnel and into daylight. For an instant they were airborne and Kate felt sure they were about to crash.

But Ariella landed smoothly, skidding across the snow in a wide curve to slow herself down. So much snow was spraying that Kate could see nothing else. Finally, they came to a halt.

Her head was spinning, but she rolled off Ariella with a laugh. "Wow! What a ride! That was amazing!"

"Not bad, if I do say so myself," declared the snow crystal as she brushed the snow off her back with two of her arms. "I especially liked that finish."

"I thought it was *our* finish," replied Kate. "That wall came up so fast I was sure we'd be flattened."

"Not a chance," answered Ariella proudly. "I've had lots of practice entering the City at top speed."

"The City?"

"You have just entered the outermost boundary of Nel Sauria City. It's the capital of the planet Nel Sauria."

"And that ice wall—"

"Is a barrier, of course. In ancient times, before all the families of snow crystals gathered together as one People, it was used for defense. Now it just protects the City against avalanches. Since Nel Sauria is a planet at peace, we don't have any enemies to worry about." She looked suddenly grave. "At least none who live on Nel Sauria."

A chill wind passed through Kate, but not from the snows surrounding them. She shook herself, as one waking from a nightmare, but she couldn't completely banish the empty coldness that had suddenly touched her.

Ariella spun over to her and lightly touched her hand. "So you too know the terror of The Darkness? I am sorry."

"Is that what you call it? It was horrible! It tried to kill me! I only escaped because of my friend Morpheus."

"Your friend is very brave," said the snow crystal. "And you must be brave as well. Few have ever escaped from The Darkness, and none without a great battle."

"Our battle ended only because of the avalanche. I may have escaped, but in the process I lost my ring and Morpheus and my only hope of finding Grandfather. Now I'll never find him!" She shook her head despondently. "What is The Darkness, anyway? What kind of thing is it? Where did it come from?"

Ariella's eyes brimmed with tears. "It came only recently to the realm of Trethoniel. And with it came the Great Trouble. That is all I know, but my mother knows more."

Kate sensed that Ariella was not telling her something. "Why does she know more?"

A large tear rolled down the crystalline face. "Because The Darkness destroyed my father."

Kate knelt down to face the snow crystal. "I'm sorry," she said, placing her cheek against Ariella's smooth face.

At length, they separated.

"I have a gift for you," said Ariella quietly. Using three arms, she swiftly dug a shallow cavity in the snow, then patted the interior until it was shaped like a smooth bowl.

Holding two of her cup-shaped hands over the bowl, she clapped them together loudly. Instantly, a clear liquid began to pour from them, sparkling brightly as it cascaded down to form a glistening pool.

"For you who have entered The Darkness and survived, I give you a few drops of the most cleansing substance in the universe. It is the pure essence of Trethoniel's liquid crystals. On your planet, you might call it *mountain spring water*. But unlike water, it will not freeze. You may wash yourself with it if you choose . . .

but remember, a little will go a long way."

Without hesitation, Kate thrust her hands and face into the cleansing liquid. It was cold and fresh and bracing, like the tarns of Scotland where she had gone swimming with Grandfather—but better. Instantly, she felt cleaner. And something more: As her body drank deeply of the essence, she felt somehow stronger, somehow fortified. She untied her braid and scrubbed her hair vigorously. Then she pulled off her sweatshirt and jeans and rinsed herself thoroughly. From top to bottom she rubbed in the sparkling liquid, including behind her ears and under her fingernails and toenails. Her entire self tingled, as though she had just stepped out of an old and withered layer of skin. Finally, she wrung out her clothes and rinsed them in the crystal essence.

"It feels so good to be clean!" she exclaimed as she dressed herself again. "I've never needed a bath so badly in my life."

"It must have been horrible inside The Darkness," said Ariella.

Kate shook her loose hair like a wet dog and began to braid it. "I don't even want to think about it again. It was . . . the worst."

"We'd better keep moving," warned Ariella. "If The Darkness missed you once, it will be searching to find you again."

"Are you sure?"

"That is its way," answered the snow crystal gravely. "But there is one place where you will be safe, one place even The Darkness cannot enter."

"Where is that?"

Ariella looked toward the far horizon and Kate's eyes followed hers. There, in the center of a large plain, were the structures of Nel Sauria City: several mounds of snow forming a series of concentric circles. In the center of the innermost circle gleamed a gigantic dome of solid crystal, itself large enough to house a small city. The dome radiated a rich green color, much like the eye of Morpheus but even deeper.

"What is that?"

"That is the heart of the City—indeed, the heart of Nel Sauria—the ancient crystal dome we call Broé San Sauria. The secret of how it was made has been forgotten with time, and even the true meaning of its name was lost long ago. It is the most sacred spot on all of Nel Sauria. Most of the residents of the City live in the mounds you can see surrounding the dome, except for the Triangles, who prefer their nests upon the high ridges."

"And what happens in the green dome—Broé whatever-you-call-it?"

Ariella's eyes gleamed proudly. "Broé San Sauria is where the Nurse Crystals do their healing work, and where our young crystals are born. That is where we will find my mother."

Turning to Ariella, Kate asked: "Are you a Nurse Crystal?"

The snow crystal laughed like the pealing of bells. "No," she said, "although someday I hope to be one. My training has barely begun. A true Nurse Crystal has powers beyond anything you could imagine."

Kate studied the dome, glistening brightly in the distance. Broé San Sauria seemed totally protected and peaceful, a place where she could be truly safe, at last.

Then her eyes fell to her hand, to the empty spot on her finger where the butterfly ring had once rested.

Where was it now? Where was Morpheus? And, most importantly, where was Grandfather?

"Let's go," said Ariella.

Kate hesitated. "If I go with you, I'm sure I'll be safe and warm . . ."

"That's right. But if you don't come soon, The Darkness is sure to reappear."

Kate still didn't budge.

"What's wrong, Kate? Are you afraid of something?"

Her eyes lifted to the glistening white ridge rising in the distance. "If I go with you, I know I'll be safe, but unless I find my ring soon . . . I know Grandfather's out there someplace—trying to find a way to save the Sun— our star. He could be in serious trouble. The Darkness might attack him! I've got to warn him. I've got to find him. And the only way to do that is to find my ring first."

Ariella gave her a puzzled look. "I don't understand. What's wrong with taking a little time to rest before you go out searching for your ring? You've been through a lot."

"My ring has barely half its time left, that's what's wrong! I don't know whether it keeps losing PCL— that's its source of energy—even when it's not on my hand . . . but I *do* know that Grandfather's ring has even less time left. He might be out of PCL already, for all I know." She touched one of Ariella's arms. "I know The Darkness is out there someplace, but so is Grandfather. I can feel it."

"But you might never find your ring under all that snow!"

Kate's eyes roamed across the fields of white that

seemed to stretch endlessly in all directions, then returned to Ariella. "I've got to try."

Ariella spun still closer. "Are you really determined to do this? Broé San Sauria is so near."

"I wish I could be sure what's the right thing to do. I've never been any good at making decisions. But I am sure of one thing. If Grandfather gets into trouble and I'm not there to help him, I'd never forgive myself."

"So you're going to do this crazy thing?"

"I guess so."

Ariella's eyes narrowed in concern. "Then I'm coming with you."

"No," declared Kate. "This is my problem."

"It's mine, too. After all I went through to save you, do you think I'm about to let you go back out there alone and get yourself killed? And what success do you think you'll have without a guide? You'll probably walk right into another avalanche."

"What about The Darkness? I don't want you to risk that."

"I guess I'll just hope for the best."

Kate gazed into Ariella's round eyes. "I may have lost everything else, but I think I've found a friend."

8

nimba's flight

SCANNING the enormity of the snowfields above them, Kate inhaled a deep breath of Nel Sauria's frosty air. "Whewww," she sighed, blowing a puff of mist.

Suddenly, she realized the folly of her decision. "I forgot how far we came down! It'll take so long just to get back up there. How can we possibly find my ring before Grandfather runs out of time?"

"We could spin ourselves up there in no time," suggested Ariella. She cartwheeled a short distance across the snow with amazing speed.

"Are you kidding? That only works if you have six arms! For me, that's as impossible as flying."

"You can't fly either?" asked Ariella, her eyes open to their widest. "I've never met anyone who can't either spin or fly. How do you get around on your home planet when you need to go someplace fast?"

"Rings," answered Kate grimly.

"Oh, I see," replied the snow crystal. Then she brightened and leaped high into the air above Kate. For a moment, she held herself aloft, twirling slowly, before floating back down. "If you can't fly, maybe you can leap like this. It's almost as good."

"I'm afraid not. My body's just not built for it. I guess I'll have to go one step at a time."

Kate glanced at the ridge of peaks rising high above the ice wall, swallowed hard, then started to stride off with determination. Without warning, she sunk to her thighs in the snow.

"Hey! Oh, Ariella. This is terrible!" She tried to extract herself, but the more she struggled, the more deeply she found herself swallowed by soft snow. "Help me, Ariella!"

The snow crystal spun to the edge of the expanding pit, stretched out four of her long arms, and tried to pull Kate free. The snow was now nearly up to her shoulders. Several times Ariella came close to retrieving her, only to have the soft snow break through again.

A wave of fear shot through Kate, and her hands felt suddenly chilled. *Am I going to be buried again?*

"Small steps!" commanded Ariella. "Move slowly and take small steps!"

Kate forced herself to stay calm and to move in small, deliberate steps. Ariella was right; violent movement only made the situation worse. At last, with the crystal's help, she reached a patch of denser snow. She crawled slowly out of the pit and collapsed, breathing heavily.

"That's worse than quicksand."

"It's a soft spot," said Ariella remorsefully. "I should have warned you."

"Yes, you should have. How did the snow get like that?"

"I don't know. It's been warmer than usual recently, and soft spots are more common these days. So are avalanches. Some people think they're all tied to the Great Trouble."

"Trouble is right!" exclaimed Kate as she rose to her feet. "I've got plenty. How am I ever going to find my ring if I can't even take a step without falling in?"

Ariella's round eyes rolled skyward. "I have an idea." She began rubbing several arms together rapidly, until the vibration created a shrill, high-pitched whistle. The sound pierced the air like the cry of an angered osprey.

Kate put her hands over her ears. "What are you doing that for?"

The crystal didn't reply. She continued the vibrating motion and kept her eyes focused on one area of the sky.

Kate looked up. All she could see were banks upon banks of heavy white clouds—until a slight edge of motion appeared. Then, what looked like a piece of the clouds, triangular in shape, grew more visible. It became bigger and bigger, until suddenly Kate realized that it was descending.

The Triangle, which looked like a wing made of ice, coasted to a landing on the snow next to them. Ariella's whistling ceased and she spun to the side of the large, flat crystal.

"You called me for a good reason, I hope," growled the flying wing. "I was in the middle of an updraft, one of the best I've found in ages." His triangular eyes studied Kate suspiciously.

"Yes, Nimba," replied Ariella. "It's a good reason.

You know I never would use the distress call otherwise."

"Tell me your reason," grumbled the Triangle, "and I'll be the judge of whether it's any good or not."

"My friend here has lost her ring."

"Her what?"

"Her special ornament. It's very important to her. She needs to search for it in the high snowfields."

The rumble of a distant avalanche echoed in the chilly air. Kate turned toward the daggerlike spires of the ridge. How far above the clouds they soared she could only guess; no mountains on Earth could match their majesty. As the roar of the avalanche reverberated among the peaks, it seemed to warn her to stay away, to forget about retrieving the ring. She had escaped once, by luck. Twice would require a miracle.

Nimba's eyes flashed angrily. "You dragged me out of the sky for some silly little ornament? Just because this alien says it's important?"

Kate gathered her courage and stepped forward. "It is important. And it's not just an ornament. I need it to—to fly above the clouds. It's my only hope of finding Grandfather. He's somewhere out there—at least I think he is—searching for some way to help our Sun. He could be in trouble. And he's going to run out of time very soon!"

Nimba's pointed face twisted sharply. "That is the most unbelievable tale of woe I've heard in years. No, decades! Ariella, you should be ashamed of yourself. Dragging me out of the sky with the distress call . . . And for what? For some incredible story told by an alien!"

The Triangle shifted his stance in order to begin his

takeoff. "That's the last time any Triangle will heed your call, Ariella."

"But The Darkness is out there!" cried Kate. "It might attack Grandfather!"

Nimba froze. "How do you know about The Darkness?"

"She fought with it," declared Ariella. "She escaped, but only because she got buried by an avalanche."

"That's how I lost my ring," added Kate.

Nimba studied her closely. "The Darkness is the enemy of all living creatures. How do I know you're telling the truth? That it's not another one of your stories?"

Kate pondered for a moment. "How would I even know The Darkness exists unless it had attacked me? It's too horrible to make up."

Nimba cocked his head slightly. "That much is true. But how do I know you're not one of its spies?"

"Because I say she's not!" exclaimed Ariella. Her round eyes flashed with anger. "Don't you trust me, Nimba?"

The triangular head turned from Kate to Ariella and back again. "I do trust you, Ariella. But there is much reason for extra caution these days. The Darkness has been growing steadily more powerful, and Nel Sauria remains one of the last strongholds of resistance left. Not without great cost . . . As you know, some of our bravest defenders have fallen to The Darkness."

Ariella bowed her face slightly.

"All right," he said at last. "I'm probably just an old fool for doing this, but if you really fought with that scourge, then at least you're on the right side." He turned to Ariella and added: "And you, young one, should be staying closer to home. These are dangerous times. I was a friend of your father, and I am sure he would tell you the same."

"You were more than a friend," she answered somberly. "You were with him when he died."

"Let's get this over with," said Nimba roughly, lowering an edge of his wide wing. "Climb aboard."

Ariella spun onto Nimba's back and positioned herself in the center. Kate did her best to follow, but the crystalline body of the Triangle was as slippery as ice. Carefully, she crawled across the surface, concentrating hard to avoid sliding off.

"I'm not sure whether this is such a great idea," she said nervously to Ariella.

"Where in the high snowfields do you want to go?" asked Nimba.

"At the base of Ho Salafar Ridge, in the middle of the avalanche zone," answered Ariella. "I'll tell you when we get near." Then she turned to Kate. "Hold my arm tightly and you won't fall. Nimba's the smoothest flier on Nel Sauria, so don't worry."

"Thanks," said Kate. "But I'll keep worrying anyway. It's my nature."

"You will live longer because of it," declared Nimba. "In this case, though, you have nothing to fear. I will create a pressure pocket around you both, and that will hold you securely."

With that, the Triangle began sliding forward across the snow. Immediately, they were airborne, gliding in the direction of the great glistening peaks. Below them stretched the vast snowscape of Nel Sauria.

Kate's eyes followed the lines of white hills leading up to the main spine of the ridge, which rose like a serrated saw into the sky. "This is such a beautiful place," she said, shouting to be heard above the wind. "Especially when you don't need to walk on it. It's amazing to have a whole planet covered with snow."

"It's not," corrected Ariella. "Only the half facing away from Trethoniel is covered with snow. The other side is a single great ocean, what we call the Bottomless Blue. I've never seen it—almost nobody has—but many ancient writings tell of its beauty."

"So Nel Sauria is divided in half?"

"Yes. One half is white, the other is blue."

"But doesn't the planet rotate as it revolves around Trethoniel?"

"Rotate?" Ariella's eyes assumed a quizzical look. "What an odd idea! Does your Earth rotate?"

"Yes. That's how both sides get lit by the Sun, and how day and night follow each other. Say, if this snowy side of the planet is always facing away from Trethoniel, then how do you get any daylight? Why isn't it dark all the time?"

Ariella's laughter rang out, and even the wind seemed to pause and listen. "Why, from the snow, of course! Our light radiates from the snow and lights the sky. It's in the nature of the crust; a thin layer on the surface glows all the time. Do you mean to say that on your Earth it's the other way around? Your sky lights the snow?"

"I guess our snow is a lot different than yours," said Kate. "Our Sun is our only source of light. And Grandfather thinks it's about to die!"

"Did you think our snow could help?"

"No . . . but Grandfather thinks maybe Trethoniel can. That's why I'm sure he's out there someplace. He says Trethoniel is the healthiest star in the galaxy, and if he can just figure out what keeps it so healthy, maybe he can use that knowledge to help the Sun."

"Once that might have been true," said Ariella, lowering her voice so much that Kate could barely hear her above the whistling wind. "Before the Great Trouble began."

"What is this Great Trouble?" asked Kate.

"I don't really know," said Ariella. "I only know The Darkness is part of it. Other things have been happening, too."

"Like what?"

"Like that," the snow crystal answered, pointing one arm toward a gray patch of snow far below them.

At first, Kate thought Ariella was pointing to some sort of shadow, probably from a cloud. Then she realized her mistake. The gray color was part of the snow itself!

"What is it, Ariella?"

The deep pools of Ariella's eyes seemed to fill with sadness. "That was once a field of snow crops—one of the most fertile around. It used to grow tall stalks of crystalmeat, the favorite food of our People."

Examining the field more closely, Kate could see it was covered with hundreds of thousands of stiff gray stalks. They stuck out of the snow like drying bones, giving the place the feeling of an abandoned cemetery. Next to it, another snowfield was covered with pearly white stalks, but an area along its edge was also beginning to turn gray.

"What's wrong down there?" called Kate above the winds. "Is it some kind of disease?"

Ariella studied the landscape glumly. "If it is, it's no disease Nel Sauria has ever known before. Some people say it's because of the warmer temperatures. Others are sure it's something else. Nobody really knows. Not even the Sage of Sauria knows, I'm sure."

"The Sage of Sauria?"

Ariella's eyes refocused on Kate. "Oh, that's just a figure of speech. The Sage of Sauria is a legendary creature who supposedly once lived near the Bottomless Blue, but no one has seen her for thousands of years. Most people agree that she never really existed, that she's just another character out of the ancient writings."

Kate nodded. "We have characters like that on Earth. The Greek myths are full of them, and then there's Merlin and Gandalf and all the others . . . Sometimes they seem too real to be just stories, but then I realize I'm just imagining things. What was this Sage of Sauria like?"

"Very mysterious, and very wise," answered Ariella, glancing at the pinnacled ridge of peaks looming ahead of them, drawing closer by the second. "The Sage was supposed to sit for decades, motionless as a stone, watching the waters of the Bottomless Blue. Only the wisest and bravest of the ancient People tried to find her secret hideaway, in order to seek her advice, and most of them wandered for years and never found anything. Of the lucky few who found the way, most of them could not understand the meaning of the Sage's riddles, or could not remember them when they returned." She paused thoughtfully. "You are very brave yourself, Kate, to journey all the way to Trethoniel."

"Not really. I just worry a lot. If I hadn't been scared by a ghost, I'd probably never be here."

"I've never seen Trethoniel myself," said the snow crystal. "I've read many writings about it, though. I'm sure it's every bit as beautiful as the old legends say. I hope it has what you need to save your Sun."

"I do, too, but mainly I hope it has Grandfather, and that he's safe."

"There!" cried Ariella, pointing to a small hole in the snow below them. "That's where we start looking."

Like a feather on a breeze, Nimba glided to a stop near the place where Kate had been buried not long ago. His two passengers slid off his back and stood on the snow, facing him.

"Thank you," said Ariella, touching the point of his head lightly.

"We owe you a lot," added Kate.

"Don't mention it," replied the Triangle. "I hope you find your ornament before another avalanche hits." He eyed Ariella with concern. "I hope you know what you're doing. Be very careful, young one! Now, if you don't mind, I'm going to see whether that updraft is still going strong."

With a whoosh of air, Nimba was aloft. Soon he was completely invisible against the white clouds.

They began the search. Ariella spun in slow circles around the area, looking for anything unusual. Meanwhile, Kate stepped to the edge of the hole in the snow, examining it closely. Had she really dug such a deep tunnel?

The tortured black knot of the tentacle sat near her feet, marring the whiteness of the snow. She kicked it vengefully, and the snow sizzled with the impact. Foreboding as it felt to gaze into the place where she had almost perished, she knew that the ring could well be buried down there. She hesitated, then decided to try it.

Kate began to climb down into the tunnel, her heart pounding loudly. As she left the daylight behind, a sudden rush of panic seized her. What if the snow around her collapsed? Would she be buried again? Her hands grew very cold, and a chilly finger of fear ran down her spine.

She turned around, and the sight of the circle of light above helped to calm her. A few dim shafts of light drifted down to her, illuminating the tunnel's frozen walls. But her heart continued to pound with the rhythm of her fear. Then she thought of Grandfather, somewhere up there, searching . . . So too was The Darkness! She swallowed hard and forced herself to keep climbing downward.

The shaft seemed deeper than she had remembered. Then, at a certain depth, it suddenly narrowed and dropped swiftly downward in a vertical descent. Kate clung to the snowy wall and peered down into the seemingly bottomless hole.

This doesn't make sense, she told herself. *This tunnel is far too deep—and also too steep. I'd need a ladder to go down any further.*

Then she noticed a faint trace of green on the snow. The ring! She began to dig madly in the wall of the tunnel, despite how cold it made her hands, until there was a large cavity in the snow. Yet there was no further sign of the ring.

"Kate!" cried Ariella's small voice from outside the tunnel entrance. "Are you there?"

"Yes! And I think the ring is down here, too. But the tunnel is much deeper than I thought."

"Can you come up here?" called Ariella. "I think I've found something important."

Carefully, so as not to lose her footing, Kate climbed

back up to the surface. Squinting from the bright light, she looked for Ariella.

"Over here!"

She ran to join the crystal, who indicated some subtle depressions in the snow.

"They look like footprints," panted Kate. "Probably Spike's."

"That's right."

"What's so important about that? I thought you made a big discovery."

"The odd thing about these footprints," explained Ariella, "is they don't leave this area. I've searched all around, and there is no sign of Spike leaving here. Since he isn't here now, that leaves just one alternative."

"I get it!" exclaimed Kate. "So Spike went down into the tunnel—and made it deeper!" She paused thoughtfully. "But why would he go through so much trouble? Unless—"

"Unless he was going after your ring. Spike only digs when he's forced to, or when he's sure he'll find something valuable. Otherwise, he wouldn't dream of lifting an arm to dig. I'm sure he was trying to find your ring . . . and keep it for himself." Ariella's eyes darkened. "He wasn't always like that. But ever since he lost his family in the great ice wall collapse, he's been totally different. So full of bitterness. I've tried to bring him around, but it's hopeless. I'm ready to give up."

Kate pondered the gaping hole in the snow. "Grandfather said something once about PCL—about its special properties—oh, yes! He said PCL can melt through anything frozen! So if the ring was somewhere in the snow, it would have melted straight down—"

"And left a small hole behind!" finished Ariella. "That must be what Spike was following."

"As well as a green tint in the snow," added Kate. "I saw some of it myself down there." Her brow furrowed in concern. "But following Spike isn't going to be so easy. Digging straight down is one thing, but climbing straight down is another."

"No problem," declared Ariella. "Just follow me."

The six-armed crystal moved to the mouth of the tunnel and positioned herself just as if she were going to sled down it. "Climb aboard and I'll show you."

Doubtfully, Kate sat on top of her.

"Give me a push!"

"But—"

"Trust me. Now, push!"

She followed the crystal's command, and they slid over the edge. To Kate's surprise, instead of falling straight down the tunnel, they began to float slowly downward, as Ariella curved her back like a perfect parachute. Gently they drifted deeper and deeper into the great bed of snow, twirling slowly as they descended. As they passed the point where the tunnel narrowed and dropped precipitously, the circle of light shrunk into nothingness above them.

"How far down does the snow go?" asked Kate, even as the tunnel grew totally dark.

"No one knows," came the reply. "The People of the Snow have always asked that question. Many years ago, before I was born, a few brave explorers tried to find out. But none of them ever came back."

"What's that sound?"

A low, slow rumble rose to them from far below. It grew ever louder as they drifted downward, seemingly

magnified by the blackness, until it soon filled the entire
tunnel with its reverberations. Gradually it grew into a
roar, louder than all the pipes of a great cathedral organ
sounding simultaneously.

"What's that—"

Splaaash!

They landed on the surface of a surging river. Suddenly Ariella became not a parachute but a raft, with
Kate as her unwilling passenger.

"Ariella!"

Round and round they spun, as the swirling torrent
carried them deeper into the caverns of this underground
river, raging as it had raged for centuries beneath the
silent snows of Nel Sauria. Irresistibly it flowed, far below the mountains and glaciers of the surface, ultimately
to empty into the Bottomless Blue.

Onward they rode in the utter darkness of the cavern.
At one point, the roof hung so low to the river that Kate
was knocked backward and was suddenly submerged.
Ariella grabbed her by the arm and struggled to hold on,
as the cascading waters pummeled them. Numbed with
cold, Kate tried desperately to breathe, but all she got
was water. Finally, they bobbed up again and she filled
her hungry lungs with air.

"Help!" she sputtered, but the din of the terrible torrent swallowed her words.

In the blackness, they could not tell that the river had
now joined other rivers and that the cavern had widened
immensely. Mighty stalactites, pinnacles of ice stretching hundreds of feet down from the ceiling, filled the
darkened cavern like finely polished teeth.

Then, through the crashing waves, a dim light appeared. Weak and waterlogged, Kate thought it was only

her imagination. She felt heavy enough to sink, too weak
to struggle any more. Would she ever see Grandfather
again? It seemed Ariella had saved her from one death
only to join her in another.

Just then a blast of heated air struck them, as though
a great furnace door had opened in their faces. In the
same instant, the world suddenly grew bright—and Kate
realized they were falling, tumbling over the edge of an
enormous waterfall.

9

the bottomless blue

AT the top of the waterfall, Kate spied the vague outline of a twisted root dangling over the edge. She
stretched for it, grabbing hold just as the great falls emptied into the basin below.

As she caught the root with one hand, she felt it sliding through her palm. She twisted in the torrent and
reached for it with the other hand, as the force of the
cascade bounced her like a ball. The root held fast, but
her grip was tenuous.

"I'm slipping!" screamed Ariella, who was clinging
desperately to Kate's waist.

"Hold on!" cried Kate above the thunderous roar.

A sudden wave crashed against them. Kate was hurled
to the side of the waterfall, where she struck a rock wall
and lost her grip on the root. She tumbled down to a
narrow ledge protruding from the mountainside.

Amidst the spray, she lay still for a moment. Slowly,

she lifted her head, then scrambled to stand. Her ankle throbbed painfully.

"Ariella!" she called.

Her eyes followed the course of the frothing falls as it descended, falling freely for thousands of feet. Finally, it merged with a towering cloud of vapor rising from its base, and she could see no more.

Ariella was gone!

Kate slumped in a heap on the rocky ledge, mortified at her fate. She had meant to risk her own life, but not Ariella's—and now she was lost. The ring was lost. Morpheus was lost. Everything was lost.

Tears swam into her eyes, mixing with the mist of the waterfall. Suddenly she felt a searing pain in her hand.

"Ow!" she cried, jumping to her feet. "That rock is hot."

Then, for the first time, she looked beyond the spray to the landscape stretching before her. So great was her shock that for a moment she forgot about everything else. She stepped along the ledge away from the waterfall in order to get a clearer view.

There was no Bottomless Blue!

Instead of the wide blue ocean that Ariella had described, Kate could see only a roasting red desert beneath a rust-colored sky. From horizon to horizon stretched a single reach of baked rocks and burned soil. No liquid whatsoever moistened this searing cauldron, but for the seething stream of lava Kate saw pouring from one volcanic cone in the distance. Into the burning basin flowed several powerful waterfalls like the one next to her, but none was more than a mere cloud of steam by the time it ultimately reached the desert floor.

Kate lifted her eyes from this desolate landscape to

the glowing red disc above her head. Trethoniel domi-
nated the sky. It radiated powerfully, even majestically.
Yet . . . it seemed somehow different from here.

"Uhhhhh."

She whirled around. What had made that sound?

There, lying in the shadows of the rocky ledge, lay
the bent form of a snow crystal. She ran to see if it
was—

"Spike!" Kate couldn't hide her disappointment. "I
thought— I thought maybe you were Ariella."

"Uhhhhh," moaned the crystal, struggling to sit up.
"I'm just as glad to see you, Alien."

Moving closer, Kate could see that a portion of his
lower body was missing, and a long crack wound its
way up the columnar crystal's back. She reached to help
him, but he swatted at her angrily.

"You keep your distance. It's your fault I'm here. If
you hadn't talked about your precious ring—oh! That
hurts! My only mistake was listening to you, Alien."

"I didn't mean—"

"And you've killed Ariella, too, haven't you?" Spike
tried again to sit upright, but slid back unsuccessfully.
"Ah! These sizzling rocks are going to melt me in no
time. I'll disappear just like the ocean did—if it ever
existed. I never should have listened to those stupid fairy
tales!"

"Don't you want some help?" asked Kate. "Maybe I
can help you if you'll let me."

"Not on your life. Don't touch me." He groaned painfully. "What's the use? I'm not going to last much
longer—in this heat."

"Are you really melting? Does that mean Ariella—"

"So she did come with you! You've killed her, Alien!

Killed her for sure. Even if she made it to the valley floor alive, she's been burned to a crisp by now. Those hot rocks down there . . . this place is one big oven. Snow People can't survive in heat like this."

Kate's eyes again filled with tears. "I didn't mean to hurt her," she said sorrowfully. "I didn't mean to."

"That doesn't help her much, does it? You did it to her—just like you did it to me." A look of genuine sadness filled Spike's long eyes. "It's one thing for me to die; I probably deserve to melt, anyway. But Ariella! She stood by me after everyone else had given up trying. And I never got to tell her . . ."

Kate turned away from Spike and peered over the side of the ledge. A sheer rock face dropped precipitously below them. The ledge itself, while it bent upward for some distance along the ridge, stopped completely at the waterfall. There was no route to climb down, no way to reach Ariella.

"If you're thinking about saving her, forget it!" snarled Spike. "She's long gone. You'd better—ow! Uhhhhh . . . I'm getting weaker . . . by the second. You'd better think—think about saving yourself, Alien. You're trapped here, too. I hope I live long enough to see—to see you melt."

Kate turned again to the crumpled form of the snow crystal lying on the ledge. He looked as miserable as an abandoned child: alone, lost, and frightened.

Then, to her surprise, she spotted a faint outline of something on the rock wall above him. Was she hallucinating? It looked like some sort of carving, a petroglyph made by some ancient hand.

She moved sideways to see if a different angle made the image any clearer. There, indeed, she saw carved into the stone the unmistakable shape of a six-sided snow crystal.

"What are you staring at, Alien?"

"A carving in the rock! It looks like Ariella!"

"You're seeing things."

"No, I'm not. It's there!" She started to run her finger along the deep indentation, but the heat of the rock repelled her. "Somebody carved it. I'm sure of it. That means somebody else has been here! Maybe one of the explorers Ariella spoke about. Either they came here the same way we did—or there's some other route."

"Give up, Alien! Your brain is already—already melting. You'll never get . . . out of here, and neither will I. We're both going to—ah! oh!—roast to death! Already . . . I feel weaker, weaker all the time. I'm never . . . never . . ."

With that, he fell silent.

Kate wiped the perspiration from her face. She had to find a way out of here. She studied the line of the ledge as it climbed along the rocky cliff. No doubt this cliff was just on the other side of the mountains from the snowfields where she had landed. But it seemed like another planet. Perhaps the ledge was actually made by someone . . . someone long ago. Perhaps it was once a trail! To the waterfall, perhaps? But why would anyone have gone through so much trouble?

She gazed at the broken body of Spike, lying motionless against the rock wall, as the striking smell of melting crystal tissue reached her nose. It was as fresh as a spring rain, and as bracing as the bath Ariella had given her. Such a smell was utterly at odds with the desert dryness surrounding her. Again her eyes followed the long contour of the ledge until it disappeared beyond some weathered rocks.

Kate moved closer to the body. He might be alive, even though it didn't look good. If she couldn't help Ariella, and she couldn't help Grandfather, at least maybe she could help somebody.

Clumsily, she lifted the limp snow crystal onto her back. He was heavier than she had thought, like a slab of tightly compressed ice from the very bottom of a glacier. She struggled to lay him across the small of her back, just as she had once seen a fireman do with an unconscious man. With one arm she held his head, with the other his broken base.

Hunched over from her heavy load, Kate started to walk along the ledge. Maybe, just maybe, if she could transport Spike over to the snowy side of the ridge, she could find someone who could help him. To her delight, she discovered that the ledge continued upward beyond the rock outcropping she could see from the waterfall. Still, it was very rough going: The would-be trail was strewn with broken bits of stones and unforgiving pits. In the sweltering heat, Kate frequently had to stop and lift one hand to her brow—without losing her hold on Spike—to wipe away the perspiration that stung her eyes.

Her ankle pained her with every step, and she tried to favor the other foot. As she lifted her load over one particularly large stone, however, she twisted it slightly.

"Ow!" she cried, dropping Spike's body and collapsing on top of it. She burned her hand again on the hot rocks as she fell, and her ankle throbbed painfully. Tears brewed, blurring her vision, but she forced them back.

She picked herself up and tried again to lift her cum-

bersome load. With considerable effort, she placed
Spike's body back in position and continued to trudge
slowly onward.

Recalling some words Grandfather had once chanted
as they hiked over a difficult trail in Scotland, she began
to repeat them over and over. *Light as a feather, strong
as an ox. Light as a feather, strong as an ox.* At first
the words made her feel slightly stronger, but soon they
seemed as heavy as the body on her back, and she
stopped saying the chant.

Slowly, she ascended the side of the ridge. At one
point, the ledge suddenly narrowed into a thin shelf,
barely six inches wide. Kate tried not to look down, but
her memory of the sheer drop below was only too clear.

She hesitated, then glanced behind her toward the waterfall, which was now invisible but for the spiraling
tower of mist. She was used to being alone, but this was
more alone than she had ever been. She thought of Ariella, dear Ariella, and of Morpheus, who fought so valiantly to save her. She thought of Mom and Dad—so
willing to let her be herself, difficult as she could be
sometimes, and of Cumberland, her loyal friend who
never asked for anything in return. And she thought of
Grandfather—oh, Grandfather! Would she ever see any
of them again?

Gathering herself, she stepped carefully across the
stretch as if it were a slippery log spanning a roaring
river. As she reached the other side, she heaved a sigh
of relief and mopped her sweaty brow.

Then she saw the crevasse.

A few steps ahead, the rock-strewn ledge divided, as
if a fault line had severed the entire mountainside. The
resulting gap, more than five feet across, was so deep

that she could see nothing but darkness in its shadowy depths.

Light as a feather, strong as an ox, she told herself weakly. *Light as a feather, strong as an ox.*

Kate moved cautiously to the edge. Swinging Spike's body around, she positioned it like an ungainly sack against her shoulder. With an enormous heave, she threw her load to the opposite side. It landed with a thud on the rocks.

Once again Kate looked backward. The waterfall seemed so far away, and yet the top of the ridge seemed even farther. Where was she going, anyway? She wondered whether all this effort would lead only to another impassable crevasse.

Feeling weaker then she had ever felt, she bent forward to stretch her back. Her ankle hurt so much. The swelling was growing worse. Her braid fell over her shoulder, rubbing against her cheek. Kate suddenly remembered the way Grandfather used to run his hand along her braid, one of his gestures that said more than any amount of words.

Kate again eyed the yawning chasm. Her heart pounded. With a deep breath, she limped toward the edge, planted her good foot, and leaped with all her strength.

Made it!

She clung to a jagged rock and pulled herself clear of the crevasse. It was all she could do to lift Spike's heavy body into the fireman's carry again. Her swollen ankle ached and her steps grew increasingly wobbly as she climbed higher and higher on the rocky slope, but she pressed on.

At last, the ledge turned into an uneven trail, which

ran like a ribbon over the ridge. By now Kate's head
was so heavy that she could not lift it to see what lay
ahead: It was all she could do to make one foot move
in front of the other.

A gust of cold air hit her, so suddenly that she lost
her balance and fell on the side of the trail. To her
amazement, gleaming white peaks towered above her
left and right sides. Patches of snow were all around.
She had reached the top of the ridge!

Kate found herself sitting on a low pass dividing the
knife-edge ridge that separated a world of red desolation
from a world of creamy white cornices. The trail continued over the ridge to a large snowfield below, where
it disappeared from view. She raised her face toward the
peaks and drank deeply of the rich mountain air. The
wind felt cool against her sweaty face.

Her eye fell to Spike, lying as still as death on the
rocks by a snowdrift. He had been right; she had caused
Ariella's death. Nothing could ever assuage that pain.

Some very strange things were happening to this
planet, things she couldn't fully comprehend. The Great
Trouble was more a mystery than ever. Perhaps there
was some connection between The Darkness, the soft
spots, and the fields of dying crystalmeat. But what
could have transformed the Bottomless Blue into a searing desert? How could all these things be happening under the very nose of the most beautiful star in the
galaxy?

Earth, that sparkling blue sapphire she had seen from
her perch upon Morpheus, now seemed so very far
away. How she longed to glimpse it again, to feel its
soil underfoot and its air overhead. To smell the chrysanthemums in the garden. To run through the old apple

orchard, to swim in the pond behind Grandfather's house, to play with Cumberland . . . oh, Cumberland!

Spying a large, snow-crusted rock sitting near the trail, Kate thought it would be a good place to ponder her fate, and Grandfather's. She had given up any hope of finding him; he would never even know how hard she had tried. Only Ariella and Morpheus knew, and they were lost forever.

Dejectedly, she hobbled over to the rock and started to climb it. Then, without warning, the rock moved.

10

strange encounters

KATE tumbled backward onto the snow-dappled ridge as the great rock stirred. Then came a deep rumble that she felt through to the marrow of her bones, and the rock shifted, heaved, and finally started to roll over.

With a gasp, Kate realized that the underside of the rock was coated with some form of densely matted fur. It looked silver in color, although it could actually have been white beneath the layers of finely crushed stones that clung tightly to it. What she had taken for patches of snow on top of the rock were, in fact, more of this rough fur. As the rock rolled onto its side, it began to lengthen and widen, stretching itself like an enormous hedgehog uncurling before Kate's eyes.

The stretching continued until sharp corners began to appear on the surface of the rock, now standing three times as tall as Kate. Soon the rock's front, back, and sides were covered with a precise array of angles and facets. As the rough face of the rock was replaced by these crystalline corners, it grew smooth, even shiny, except for the splotches of shaggy fur draping over the facets.

Then Kate noticed one thing more: In the center of the crystal sat a single round eye, as blue as the deepest ocean. Its piercing gaze was trained directly on her.

As suddenly as it had started, the rumbling ceased. The great rock, now no longer a rock but a giant do-decahedral crystal, sat motionless atop the ridge, its contours no less imposing than the gleaming peaks behind it.

Kate was too frightened to move. All she could do was to stare helplessly at the unblinking blue eye of the enormous, shaggy crystal whose breadth now blocked the light of Trethoniel, leaving her in shadow. She knew that she was being carefully examined, just as a small fish is examined by a giant polar bear before the bear pounces on it, crushing it to death between its powerful jaws.

"Fear . . . me . . . not."

The words shook the ground like an earthquake. "Fear me not, unless you fear the truth."

Slowly, Kate regained her feet. She stood in awe, not daring to step any nearer to this strange beast that had sprung so unexpectedly from the mountain tundra, and not daring to run away. Mustering her courage, she forced herself to speak. "I don't fear the truth. I only fear The Darkness and the loss of people I love."

The great crystal stirred, grinding together the stones beneath its massive body. Then it spoke again, in a voice as rough as a landslide pouring over a slope. "You have chosen well your fears. Who are you and how did you come to Nel Sauria?"

Kate stood as motionless as the mountains surrounding her and drew in a deep breath. "I am Kate Prancer Gordon, from the planet Earth. I came here searching for Grandfather, but now I'll never find him. There's no hope."

Again the giant crystal stirred, crushing the rocks beneath it. "Hope is like a shadow, not easily lost."

Unsure what to make of this comment, or of the shaggy crystal itself, Kate could only ask: "What do you mean?"

"Your search may have ended," rumbled the huge crystal, "but your struggle has barely begun."

"How can you say that? You don't know what I've been through!"

"To live is to struggle," the shaggy being declared. "To seek is to find."

"Find what? Are you telling me I'm going to find something?"

"I am telling you," the crystal replied in its stone-grinding voice, "that I have seen the one you search for."

Fireworks exploded inside Kate. "What? You saw Grandfather?"

"A single eye can see many things," answered the giant crystal.

With those words, the crystal's deep blue eye suddenly flashed with light, like a signal mirror reflecting the Sun. Kate's hunger to find Grandfather, now fully rekindled, overpowered her fears. She stepped closer to the great crystal.

"Tell me what you saw!" she pleaded. "Is he in trouble? Is he hurt?"

The crystal made no sound. Only the round eye, glowing strangely, showed any sign of life. Across it swirled a whirlpool of undefined shapes and colors.

Then the shapes coalesced into a sharp image. A single yellow star, shining powerfully, filled the eye. *Could that be the Sun?* wondered Kate, studying the image closely.

Without any warning, the star faltered, faded, and suddenly collapsed into a pinpoint of light. Then, as Kate shuddered, it disappeared completely, leaving behind only an empty sector of space. Nothing at all remained to show that once a star had been there, burning brightly.

Before Kate could ask any questions, the eye swirled again and swiftly evolved into a new image. It was a mighty red star, surrounded by a nebula of colorful gases. There could be no mistake about its identity; Kate had come to know it well. She momentarily forgot about the death of the yellow star, as the radiant beauty of Trethoniel touched her again with wonder. She could almost hear the distant strains of its timeless music floating across the heavens.

Then a sense of dread filled her as she discerned a darkened shape moving into view. Long and writhing, its body slowly swam across the brilliant face of Trethoniel, blocking its light completely. Kate released a cry of fear and pain, and instantly the eye went dark.

"Why did you show me The Darkness?" she demanded. "Where is Grandfather? I thought you were going to show me Grandfather!"

The great crystal again shifted its weight on the ridge, as the eye's deep blue color returned. "I said only that I have seen the one you search for," rumbled the reply. "It is possible, in time, that you will see what I have seen. But first you must understand a basic truth."

"What truth?"

"There are two kinds of death for a star, and they are as different as hope is different from despair."

"Different?" Kate cocked her head in puzzlement. "I don't get it. Death is death, isn't it? Anyway, what does all this have to do with Grandfather? Are you telling me that's the Sun's future? Or Grandfather's future?"

Grinding more stones into the ground, the crystal spoke solemnly. "The future cannot be read, for it waits to be written."

"Then why did you show all that to me?" Kate's voice was cracking with exasperation. "I don't need to know the future! I only want to find Grandfather!"

"To find him may be one thing, to save him another." The ominous words of the great crystal hung heavily upon the air.

"Save him?" asked Kate. "From what?"

"To save him you must trust that life and death are both seasons of the Pattern. If you trust in the Pattern, you trust in yourself. And if you trust in yourself, your voice holds all the power of truth."

"But why does he need to be saved?" demanded Kate.

The shaggy crystal made no effort to respond.

Kate shook her head in dismay. "Now I know who you really are! Ariella thought you were just a legend . . . but even in the legend nobody could understand your riddles." She moved back a few paces so she could see all of the mammoth being. "You said you might show him to me. Please! Won't you help me?" she cried, arms outstretched. "Won't you help me find Grandfather?"

As if in answer, the Sage of Sauria began to shake violently. A great rumble shook the ridge, and soon the sharp edges of her many facets became blurred and rough-hewn. Her round blue eye closed tightly. Meanwhile, her entire body began to shrink steadily in size until, at last, the Sage of Sauria resembled nothing more than a large rock with several patches of snow encrusting its surface.

"No!" shouted Kate above the tremor. "Don't go! I need your h—"

Suddenly, she caught sight of a dark form emerging from the clouds above. A wave of terror shot through her. *The Darkness. It's come back.*

She ran to the Sage of Sauria, now just an appendage of the rocky ridge, and struck forcefully with her fist. The pain in her hand was dwarfed by the pain in her heart: The rocklike being didn't budge. Like a turtle seeking protection inside its shell, the Sage of Sauria had abandoned her.

Kate scanned the ridge madly, looking for any place to hide. There was none to be seen. Again, she glanced skyward.

At that instant, she realized her mistake.

"Grandfather!"

Diving through the clouds came Orpheus, twin brother of Morpheus, with Grandfather leaning forward like a jockey urging his horse on to maximum speed. With a swoop of iridescent wings, they glided to a landing on the snow-crusted rocks next to Kate.

"Grandfather!" she cried again.

"Kaitlyn!" came the reply.

They ran to each other and embraced. Then Grandfather fell backward into a drift, pulling Kate down with him.

"Oh, Grandfather! I thought—I thought I'd never see you again."

The old man shook the snow from his hair. "I thought I'd see you again—but on Earth! What in God's name are you doing here?"

"I followed you! I was so afraid you might—"

"Get into trouble?" Grandfather's bushy eyebrows climbed high on his forehead as his amazement now mixed with amusement. "Ah, you clever little creature. Just couldn't bear to see me get myself lost in some far corner of the galaxy, could you?"

"Right! I was so worried about you . . . I just had to make sure you were safe." She tried to frown sternly. "I couldn't believe you broke your most solemn promise."

"Yes, well . . . I had to do it, Kaitlyn. Please forgive me. The Sun is in such peril."

"I forgive you," smiled Kate. "I just hope God does, too."

"God is very forgiving of Oxford men," he replied with a twinkle. "You found the other ring, didn't you?"

"Yes," answered Kate, suddenly somber. "But . . ."

The old man paid no heed to her change of mood. "Didn't you realize how risky a trip like that could be? You're very lucky."

"Yes . . . but Grandfather . . ."

"I haven't been so lucky," he continued. "I've been exploring very close to the star—it's a magnificent sight to behold—and I'm more convinced than ever that Trethoniel must be the greatest source of PCL anywhere in the universe. But I haven't had any success at all in finding out how the star makes it, or how the Sun could make more. Meanwhile, I've lost precious time. I'm starting to doubt I'm going to find out anything before it's too late."

"G-grandfather . . ." began Kate.

The old man gently stroked her long braid. "At least you're safe, dear child. I still can't believe you're really—"

He stopped himself. Grim concern filled his face and he studied her hands anxiously.

"Your ring! It's gone!"

Kate's sad eyes met his. "I know. We were attacked by The Darkness and Morpheus tried to save me, but I got caught in an avalanche and lost it!"

Grandfather stepped back, visibly shaken. "All that you've been through! I had no idea . . . Kaitlyn, it's truly a miracle that you survived. Not only must this planet have an oxygen-based atmosphere, but you could easily have frozen to death under a mountain of snow."

"I nearly did," she replied. "I don't know how I ever dug myself out. I just kept wondering if you were in trouble, and—oh, Grandfather! I'm so glad to see you."

The old man held his granddaughter for a long moment, as the winds whirled across the snowy ridge.

"I still don't understand why you didn't freeze to death," said the old astronomer, wiping the tears from her cheek.

"I would have," she replied, "if it hadn't been for Ariella. She saved my life."

Grandfather then noticed the small crystalline figure lying on the rocks a few paces away.

"Heavens," he said in wonder. "Is that her?"

"No! That's Spike, and he's not anything like her! She's . . ." Her voice faded into silence.

"She's what, Kaitlyn?"

"She's dead. Melted. She went over the waterfall into that horrible desert. And it's all my fault! So I lost her and the ring—and Morpheus, too."

"My brother," moaned Orpheus, shaking his antennae violently. His enormous green eyes gave Kate a look of unbearable pain.

"I'm sorry," said Kate sadly.

The butterfly waved his antennae dejectedly.

Grandfather frowned. "Until the ring is touched again by a living being, Morpheus will remain trapped inside it."

"And he was injured, wasn't he?" asked Orpheus. "I was sure that I felt him in pain."

"Yes," answered Kate, unable to look directly at Orpheus. "I think he was . . . hurt. It all happened so fast. The Darkness hit him with its tail and I don't know what happened after that."

Orpheus' body trembled. Grandfather laid his hand gently on the butterfly's neck, which seemed to calm him a little.

"A creature such as you describe must be a very powerful source of anti-light—very powerful, indeed—to separate you from your butterfly," said Grandfather grimly. "I might have missed some random elements in making the PCL, but that still wouldn't account for what happened. No, there's something strange abroad in Trethoniel."

"Yes," exclaimed Kate. "And that's not all that's strange. Right here on—"

"Orpheus!" Grandfather's cry interrupted her. "Orpheus, calm down!"

The great butterfly suddenly reared back, swaying his antennae furiously. "I must fly!" he cried.

Grandfather tried to restrain him, but without success.

The Darkness is near, thought Kate. Once again she felt the touch of utter coldness, and for the first time since she had donned Ariella's cloak of crystalline light, her whole body felt chilled.

"Stop, Orpheus!"

At that instant, the butterfly broke free of Grandfather's grip and lifted off toward one of the high peaks along the ridge.

"Come back," called Grandfather. "Come back!"

But Orpheus ignored his command.

"Orpheus! Come back!" Grandfather kicked angrily at the snow. "Damn that random element. I should never have—what in heaven's name—"

Just as Orpheus was about to disappear behind a cornice of snow, the great butterfly did something very strange.

"Somersaults!" cried Kate. "He's turning somersaults in the air."

As they stared in amazement, another pair of flashing wings appeared over the edge of the wall.

"Morpheus!"

"But how?"

Together, the two brothers celebrated their reunion in the finest tradition of aerial gymnastics. Somersaults, spins, loop-de-loops, and rolling turns decorated the sky. At last, they sailed down to the ridge next to Grandfather and Kate, landing with only a whisper of wind.

"Morpheus!" cried Kate, as she rushed to the great butterfly's side. "You're back!" She gently touched his left wing, which was badly frayed along its edge. "And you're hurt."

"Nothing serious," declared the butterfly. "I only hope we don't meet that creature ever again."

Kate nodded, then suddenly froze, her eyes fixed on the shape clinging to Morpheus' back.

"Ariella!"

The sparkling snow crystal leaped toward Kate and danced in the air before her face. Then she settled to the ground, and Kate gave her a hug as hearty as anyone with only two arms can deliver.

"Now I know why you wanted to find that ring." Ariella exclaimed. "I've never felt so good in my life." She then turned to Morpheus. "Those were first-class cartwheels you did up there."

The antennae quivered. "Thank you."

"I was afraid you were gone for good," Kate said.

Ariella's eyes gleamed. "So was I, especially when I realized I was melting from the heat. It's so ironic. The first time in my life I get to see our star Trethoniel, it's boiling me to death. I tried several times to climb the cliff, but it was just too steep, and much too high to jump. And those rocks were so hot! I was getting weaker by the second. So I moved back to see if I could see any kind of path or something, when suddenly I felt very faint. I fell down, and right there on the ground I saw the most beautiful little rainbow. I reached for it and the instant I touched it—this glorious creature appeared out of nowhere."

Again the antennae quivered.

"You've got the ring!" cried Kate. Then she paused. "But, Ariella, what happened to the big ocean—the Bottomless Blue?"

The snow crystal's eyes swung sadly toward the red desert. "I don't know. I don't know." Then she turned again to Kate and extended a crystalline hand. "Here. You should take this back. Rings belong to creatures who have fingers."

Kate took the butterfly ring and instantly the familiar green-blue mist filled her eyes. As she slipped it onto her finger, she felt once again the pulse of warm electricity coursing through her. Even as her body vanished, it was replaced with a clearer, lighter version of herself.

Her eyes met Grandfather's. "I had almost forgotten how wonderful it feels."

The astronomer stepped toward Ariella and bent down on one knee. "Dear creature, I know you are the one who saved my Kaitlyn's life. I thank you. I thank you with all my being."

"I accept your thanks," replied the snow crystal. "But I couldn't bear to let her beautiful song go silent."

Grandfather turned a puzzled face to Kate.

"I think she means the Tallis Canon. I sang it while I was digging myself out, to give me strength."

The white head nodded. "A good choice." Suddenly, he remembered something and glanced at his ring. All but half of the right wing had disintegrated. Grandfather's face grew deeply serious. "I'm afraid it's time for us to return home."

"But what about the Sun? What about the cure?"

"It's time to go, Kaitlyn. We may have a minute or so left on my ring, but with some sort of anti-light creature running loose, I don't want to take any more chances. I had no idea that there would be anything like—"

"The Darkness," completed Kate. "I didn't either. That's for sure! But are you sure you want to turn back now, when you still have a minute left? If you want to use that minute to check out something important, Grandfather, I'm ready to go with you. As long as we're careful, really careful, to avoid The Darkness, I'm willing to stay a little while longer. After all, you still might find a cure. And it's my fault you've used up a lot of time down here on Nel Sauria."

The old man eyed her lovingly. "You are very brave, Kaitlyn. That's something I didn't really know about you before this whole business began. However, it's a risk I just can't accept. If anything were to happen to you, it would be the worst thing imaginable."

"Even worse than the Sun dying?"

"Yes. That I can't control. This I can. We're going home, Kaitlyn, while we still are able. I'll have to try to do what I can in the lab to find the Sun's cure." He looked sadly toward Trethoniel. "You've been no help at all, Great Star. No help at all!"

"You may not have found a cure for the Sun," said Kate, "but you did find me. I don't know how, but I'm awfully glad you did."

Grandfather's brow wrinkled in confusion. "But it was you who found me! I mean, I heard your voice, calling to me, telling me exactly where you were."

"Me?" asked Kate, herself confused. "My voice? I was constantly calling your name, but I never really contacted you."

"That's impossible," said Grandfather, shaking his head. "I heard you, loud and clear. You directed me here."

In a flash, Kate understood. She looked knowingly toward a large, snow-crusted rock not far from where they stood, and a slight smile touched her face. "It wasn't me who contacted you, Grandfather. It was the Sage of Sauria."

Ariella spun to her side. "Are you serious? You actually met the Sage?"

Indicating the rock, Kate answered: "Yes, we met, and she told me some riddles about the Pattern. Not that I could follow any of them! Just try to climb on that rock over there, and she might do the same for you."

Ariella's eyes glowed warmly. Then, for the first time, they fell upon the broken body of Spike lying among the rocks. "Oh, Spike!" she cried, spinning over to the fallen crystal.

"I don't know if he's still alive," said Kate, "but I did my best to get him out of that oven down there."

"He's still alive," pronounced Ariella, "although just barely. You surely saved his life—poor, wretched life that it is." She gazed at the crystal sadly. "Maybe the Nurse Crystals can put him back together—physically, at least. But I don't think anyone can ever heal the bitterness that infected him when he lost his family. I'm afraid the Spike I once knew is gone forever."

Kate reached for one of Ariella's cupped hands and held it in her own. "You may not be able to change Spike's life, but you've definitely changed mine. I don't know how to thank you."

The snow crystal brightened. "By staying a while longer."

Kate looked hopefully at Grandfather, who shook his head resolutely. She faced Ariella again and whispered, "I guess this means goodbye. I really wish I could give you something special, after all you've given me."

Ariella's eyes sparkled. "Someday, perhaps, you will

come back to Nel Sauria and teach me the words to that song."

"And I'll make you some hot chocolate, too," added Kate with a sad smile.

"But not now," declared Grandfather. "Now we must fly. I'm worried that The Darkness, as you call it, is still nearby."

Reluctantly, Kate gave the snow crystal a parting hug. "I will miss you."

"And I will miss you."

"Kaitlyn!" called Grandfather, who was already astride Orpheus. "Let's go!"

She walked slowly over to Morpheus, who had straightened his antennae in readiness for their long voyage. He bent lower so that she could climb aboard easily.

"To Earth, then," commanded Grandfather.

"Goodbye, Ariella!"

With a blur of iridescent blue, the great butterflies lifted off together, beating their wings furiously. Before Ariella could utter the word goodbye, they had disappeared into the clouds.

11

earthbound

As they sailed through the atmosphere of Nel Sauria, the vividly colored nebula of Trethoniel wove its way across the starscape. The great red giant itself, glowing as incandescent as ever, seemed to stretch out long arms of light to them, beckoning them to stay.

"We'll be home in no time," said Grandfather, his white hair glistening in the starlight. "Perhaps that cup of tea I asked you to make will still be warm."

To her own surprise, Kate felt more sad than relieved to hear his words. She cast a glance behind them toward the planet Nel Sauria, perfectly white from this angle, receding rapidly in the distance.

"I know it's difficult to leave," said Grandfather, hearing her thoughts. "We've been treated to an experience that no one else on Earth has ever known."

"Or will ever know, unless you can cure the Sun's problems," replied Kate. She continued to gaze at the small white planet, then added wistfully: "I'm really going to miss Ariella."

"You two actually came to know each other a little bit, didn't you?"

Kate made no answer, but deep inside of herself she knew that she had just made—and lost—her first true friend, other than Grandfather.

Suddenly, both butterflies lurched forward, nearly dislodging their passengers.

"Orpheus! Morpheus!" commanded Grandfather. "What do you think you're doing? This is no time for games. Take us to Earth!"

"I—I'm trying," said Orpheus, his antennae quivering with stress.

"I feel so—so weak all of a sudden," moaned Morpheus. "I—just—can't push myself—any—faster."

"We're slowing down!"

Even as Kate cried out, the wings of their interstellar steeds began to beat less and less vigorously. Soon they were no longer a blur of motion, but were clearly visible, flapping strenuously in the void of space.

"What's wrong?" cried Grandfather. "Is something pulling you back?"

"No," panted Orpheus. "My—strength is being—being sapped."

Kate clutched Morpheus' neck more tightly. She looked toward Grandfather, whose eyes were filled with fear.

"That's impossible!" he protested. "We should have plenty of time left."

"But we don't!" groaned Morpheus. "Something—is blocking—the PCL I need! It's—draining—me!"

Grandfather shook his head in disbelief. "I don't understand. Something must be interfering with the conductive property of the rings!"

Kate looked at her butterfly ring. A good portion of the right wing remained; Morpheus should still have plenty of fuel. Then she noticed something else, something that made her gasp: The ring was steadily losing its luster. Before her eyes, its iridescent gleam faded and hardened into a dense, dull gray, as if it had turned into stone.

Even as the butterflies strained to move ahead, their wings grew steadily thinner, lighter, until they looked like faded reflections of themselves. Patches of the wings became invisible, so Kate could see only empty blackness where once she saw iridescent blues and greens.

"There," called Morpheus, his antennae indicating a flat, rectangular crystal, barely big enough to hold the two butterflies, floating to the left of them. "We—must—land—there."

"I can go—no further," moaned Orpheus, his entire body shivering with exhaustion. "I can't—can't make it."

"It's not far," cried Morpheus. "You—can—do it."

Ghosts of their former selves, Morpheus and Orpheus struggled to bring themselves and their passengers closer to the rectangular crystal. With a wrenching effort of their nearly transparent wings, they finally pulled near to the edge. Then, giving one last push, they toppled over onto the crystal, sending Kate and Grandfather skidding across its smooth, glassy surface.

Exhausted, the great butterflies lay prone on the crystal, legs splayed, breathing heavily. Slowly, to Kate's horror, their wings grew more and more transparent until, finally, they could no longer be seen.

"Morpheus! Your wings!"

The antennae quivered weakly. "I am—fading, Kate.
I can't—"

"Morpheus!" she cried. "Come back!"

Grandfather stepped over to her side. Like the butterflies, his eyes also seemed drained of light. He watched
helplessly as the two black bodies slowly faded away
entirely. The last thing to disappear was one of Morpheus' antennae, which quivered valiantly before it vanished.

"What happened, Grandfather? Can't you fix it? The
rings had plenty of PCL left: You said so. You said so.
Now we're dead for sure!"

Kate stepped to the edge of the flat crystal and peered
dismally over the edge. "Stranded . . . just waiting for
The Darkness to come and get us. We should have
stayed down there with Ariella." She turned again to
Grandfather, and in a fearful whisper, she asked:
"What's going to happen now?"

Grandfather heaved a painful sigh. "I don't know,
Kaitlyn. I don't know." He studied the dull half-wing on
the turquoise band around his finger. "I don't even know
what's happened to our rings. Something's blocking
their conductivity. We're still made of heartlight, or else
we'd be dead already, frozen, suffocated and irradiated
to boot. Somehow the rings still have enough power to
keep our heartlights intact, but not enough to bring the
butterflies to life. It doesn't make any sense!"

He brushed a clump of hair off his forehead and focused his regretful eyes on Kate. "Never—not even in
my worst dreams—did I think that I would end up putting your life at risk. I should never have made a second
ring. My own life is one thing . . . but yours."

He spun around to face the shining red mass of Tre-thoniel. Raising his fist, he shouted: "I came here for an answer! I came here for help! And what have you given me? The worst disaster I could ever imagine!"

Dejectedly, he looked at his own reflection in the mir-rorlike crystal. "It's my own fault, not Trethoniel's. I'm such a stupid old fool. I never expected that Trethoniel's gift would be death instead of life . . . And I must have botched the formula for making PCL. What a worthless excuse for a scientist I am."

Kate felt a surge of sympathy for him. How could he have known the rings would fail? He never wanted her to come along in the first place: That was her own idea. He wasn't to blame for that. All he had ever wanted was to stop the Sun from destroying itself—and life on Earth in the process.

She moved to his side and touched his arm. "It's not your fault. It's not anyone's fault, really." She laid her head against his white lab coat. "Until this second I never really believed—down inside, I mean—that the Sun would die, and the Earth would die, and we would die. I guess I always thought you'd find an answer some-how. Oh, Grandfather! Now I'm so scared."

Two bushy eyebrows lifted hesitantly, as if to say: "So am I."

Wordlessly, they gazed across the starscape of Tre-thoniel, watching the shifting, seamless sea of colors. Bursts of bright light and floating crystals seemed to dance around them in an elegant minuet. Stellar winds buffeted them, tousling Grandfather's white hair.

Gently, he put his hand upon Kate's shoulder. Despite everything, the two lost voyagers felt nudged by a grow-ing awareness of the immense beauty surrounding them.

"Whatever happens," said Kate softly, "I'm glad I got to see this." She looked up at Grandfather. "And if something bad has to happen to us, I'd rather it happen while we're together."

"So would I, Kaitlyn." He stroked her braid tenderly. "I just didn't think it would happen like this. Or so soon! I suppose this is just a lesson in how small and unimportant we are in the grand scheme of things."

"But you're always telling me how every living thing is important."

"Right you are," replied the old man. "Thank you for reminding me. Every piece of the universe, even the tiniest little snow crystal, matters somehow. We can't forget that. I have a place in the Pattern, and you do, too. An important place."

Kate frowned. "I still have trouble swallowing all that."

"Why?"

"I just don't—I just don't feel like I matter much to the universe, that's all. Morpheus tried to tell me the same thing. I know I matter to you, and to Mom and Dad, and maybe to Ariella—but that's different. Why do I really matter to anything else?"

Grandfather shrugged despondently. "I suppose—"

A violent jolt interrupted him.

"Hey!" shrieked Kate. "The crystal! It's moving!"

"My God!"

12

the voice

As they held each other tightly, the mirrorlike crystal on which they stood began to buzz with vibrations. Slowly, its once-defined edges became silvery blurs and began to curl upward around them.

With every passing second, the vibrating grew more intense, until they could barely stand upright. The sea of floating crystals was now just a blur.

"We're trapped!" screamed Kate, as the rim of the crystal closed around them.

"Dear God!" exclaimed Grandfather.

The vibrations increased to the point where Grandfather and Kate toppled over in a pile. As the crystalline mass extended itself, the hollow in the middle where they stood began to deepen, like a bowl. At the same time, the crystal grew more and more clear, until finally it was perfectly transparent. Eventually, the edges joined above them in a seamless unity.

Suddenly, the vibrations ceased.

Slowly, cautiously, they regained their feet.

"It's a globe," said Kate, incredulous. "A big globe."

Indeed, they found themselves standing inside a large, transparent sphere. The great sea of mist around them whistled ominously.

"I'm scared," said Kate.

Then came the Voice.

From all around them, made from the deepest tones in the universe, came a bass-bass voice. It sounded as if someone had begun to play a titanic cello, whose strings were as long as a galaxy, and whose reverberations rolled out of a bottomless black hole.

"You need not fear." The words echoed across the starscape. *"I am the Voice of Trethoniel."*

Trying to regain his composure, Grandfather stood erect and tall in the middle of the great globe. He bowed slowly and respectfully.

Kate glanced at him worriedly. How could they be sure this was really the voice of the star? How could they know it was not really The Darkness or some other nightmarish creature?

"I am glad you have arrived. I am glad you have come to me," rumbled the Voice like a thundering storm.

"We are glad to be here," Grandfather replied, with more than a touch of fear in his voice. "I am Doctor Miles Prancer of the planet Earth, and this is my granddaughter Kaitlyn."

"You have come just in time," reverberated the reply.

"Yes," answered Grandfather. "How did you know? Our Sun is on the edge of—"

"No!" bellowed the Voice. "I speak not of your Sun. You have come just in time to save another star."

"Another star?" Grandfather's brow furrowed. "What star is that?"

The winds swept around the globe before the Voice spoke again, answering the question with a single word: "Trethoniel."

"Help Trethoniel?" cried Kate. "Are you really in danger? Is it because of The Darkness?"

"Patience, young one," commanded the Voice. "At the appropriate time, everything will be explained to you. If Trethoniel can be rescued from its current danger, it may even be possible to save that insignificant star you call the Sun. A strong Trethoniel can do many things. First, however, you must prove your worth by helping me."

"It may be insignificant to you," protested Kate, "but it's the only Sun we have. And we don't have much time!"

"You have time enough to help Trethoniel. My need is far greater than yours."

"But—"

"Quiet, Kate!" said Grandfather, squeezing her hand. "How can we help you, Great Star?"

"Soon enough, I shall explain. All you need to know is that the music of Trethoniel is in grave danger."

What kind of danger? wondered Kate. From The Darkness? From the same disease that had stricken the Sun? She had hoped that Trethoniel would harbor the solution to their problems. Why then did this voice make her feel so afraid?

She turned anxiously to Grandfather. He stood in rapt attention, lost in thought. His face showed great anticipation, as if a long-awaited dream had finally come true.

A deep, full laughter rolled through the mists like a

tsunami. "The young one does not yet believe I am Tre-thoniel."

Grandfather looked at Kate with surprise. She squeezed his hand fearfully.

The Voice came again, but more gently this time. "Very good. Such independence is one reason your little species has survived as long as it has, despite its other qualities." Then it grew serious, almost threatening. "But I am what I say I am. I do not have time to explain myself to small minds. And I hold you both as mere specks of dust in a bubble of my own creation."

"Kate," whispered Grandfather urgently. "Don't upset the star. It may be quick to anger, and its anger could be terrible. Remember that without our butterflies we have no escape!"

"But—" Kate objected faintly. "I was just feeling—"

"Feeling what?"

She looked into Grandfather's eyes. "I don't know exactly. Afraid, I guess."

Grandfather pulled her nearer. "Don't worry, Kaitlyn. I'll do what is best for us. You know I will."

He turned to the swirling mist. "She is only a child," he apologized. "She means no harm to Trethoniel."

They waited for a reply, but no reply came. Instead, a strange tenseness filled the air, a tenseness which brewed and bubbled until it felt like struggle, and pain. Then came a faint sound, or combination of sounds, welling up in the distance. A healing, joyous sound, like the celebration of birds at dawn's first light. Could it be? Yes! It was the music!

Then suddenly, without warning, the fair melody faded away. Deep in her chest, Kate felt again the touch of deadly coldness. She gasped. It was as if The Dark-

ness had just flown past, brushing her heart with its poisonous tail.

"The music!" she cried. "Bring it back!"

"I am trying," declared the Voice, its unfathomably
deep tones weighed down by an ancient sadness, too old
and too immense to be comprehended by younger beings. "I am trying to save the music from total destruction."

The lovely sounds had vanished completely. All that
remained was the empty whistling of the winds.

"How can we be of service to you?" Grandfather
called into the starscape.

"I shall explain soon enough," bellowed the Voice.
"But first, I wish to show you some of my greatest marvels. I wish to show you the beauty that gives birth to
the music you have heard."

Grandfather's eyes flamed brightly. "We would be
honored to see any marvels you care to show us."

"But we have no butterflies," objected Kate meekly.
"How will we—"

"You will need no butterflies," boomed the reply. "I
shall carry you, and you shall see some of my finest
treasures. And perhaps you who are so young and full
of doubt will eventually come to show me your trust."

Kate flushed with embarrassment. "I didn't mean
to—"

A sudden jolt cut her short.

"The globe! It's moving!"

Grandfather reached for her arm and steadied her.
"Stay close to me, Kaitlyn. I know you have your doubts
. . . and so do I. But we're now at the mercy of this star,
and I don't want to upset it. It could even be Trethoniel's
energy that's keeping us alive as heartlight, now that our

rings have failed. I'm afraid we must do as it says."

"But, Grandfather—"

"No, Kate. If you don't trust the star, then at least trust me. I've made some bad mistakes, but I still know what is best for us." His eyes held hers for several seconds.

At last she lowered her gaze. "I don't know why I'm being so difficult. Maybe it was getting swallowed by The Darkness that did it. That whole experience still feels so . . . so . . . close. I'm sorry. Of course I trust you."

Grandfather's expression softened. "And I trust you. Your instincts aren't all wrong. I'm not completely comfortable with our host, either. But I know enough to be sure this is the only chance we may still have to find a way to help the Sun. And right now, we have no choice."

13

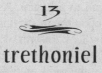

trethoniel

STANDING inside the great globe as if it were an ark, the two travelers began to sail into the billowing mists. Crystals, some gargantuan and some as small as stardust, floated past on all sides. Some of them, symmetrical and shimmering, reminded Kate of Ariella. Clouds of heated dust swirled about them, aglow with all the colors of the universe.

A gaseous shape in the distance caught her eye. It was a strange, slender cloud with dozens of long tendrils extending from its sides. As they drew nearer, she discerned that the tendrils themselves branched into smaller tendrils, and from them spouted still smaller tendrils, like thousands of misty fingers reaching out from the main stem. The entire form seemed to be dancing—bending and swaying to a rhythm older than time.

"It looks like a tree!"

Grandfather, who was studying the cloudlike being carefully, nodded in agreement.

Then the form began to metamorphose. Ever so subtly, beginning on the outermost branches, the twigs of the cloud tree began to brighten. As if a swarm of fireflies had alighted upon the misty fingers, the tip of every twig started to glow with a warm, white light. Gradually, the light seeped into the larger branches, then into the trunk, then down to the roots, until finally the whole tree radiated like a miniature star, sparkling silently in space.

Kate reached for Grandfather's hand, which had simultaneously reached out for hers. Together, they watched the glowing cloud tree dance before them.

"That is one of my oldest and finest creations," boomed the Voice, jarring them out of their reverie.

"How old is it?" asked Grandfather.

"It is nearly as old as I am, and that is more than eight billion of your Earth years."

Kate had never found it easy to comprehend such numbers. Eight billion years! And she used to think Grandfather was old.

"I resent that thought," he replied, his eyes aglow with humor. "Compared to this star, I feel like a young bobbin."

"That's the whole point! If Trethoniel is over eight billion years old, that means it's more than a hundred times . . . a hundred times . . . a hundred times a hundred times as old as you."

"You are beginning to understand, young one," boomed the Voice. "Even your rudimentary brain power has led you to the correct conclusion."

Kate stiffened. "I may not be a genius, but at least I don't pretend to know everything."

"Nothing in the universe is hidden from me," replied the Voice in an imperial tone. "Nothing in the universe is beyond my knowledge."

"Nothing at all?" asked Grandfather, an edge of sadness in his voice.

The Voice did not respond for several seconds. At last, its deep tones resonated from above and below the great globe. "You are correct, Doctor Miles Prancer of the planet Earth. Young as you are, you are wiser than I had thought. Only one thing in the entire universe is still beyond my understanding. Only one thing is still beyond my power."

"What? What is it?" asked Kate.

"In time, even you shall understand," replied the Voice.

Kate turned to Grandfather for an explanation when, suddenly, the globe began to rotate. Slowly it spun around until they were no longer facing the illuminated tree. Then, gradually, the misty curtain before them parted, revealing Trethoniel's nebula stretching far out into the galaxy. Intertwined like the threads of a timeless tapestry, the colored clouds undulated gracefully in the stellar winds. Every so often, the light from Trethoniel would catch a floating crystal and it would explode with a dazzling burst of light, shining like a jewel in the tapestry.

Kate was reminded of Morpheus and Orpheus. What had actually happened to them? Were they gone forever? But no answer came to her questions.

"Beautiful," sighed Grandfather, still captivated by the glorious vista.

"Yes, it is beautiful," declared the Voice. "On the day I was first flung to this far corner of the universe, I was nothing more than a ball of gathering gases. When all around me was empty and dark, when not a single neighboring star could be seen, I began to weave my cape of colored clouds. For many star-lives, I have spun endless crystals and painted the moving mist, even as I manufactured more light than can ever be measured. I have labored, long beyond my destined time, to create the most beautiful star in the universe."

"And you have succeeded," Grandfather added.

"No!" boomed the Voice, with such force that it shook the globe and almost knocked them off their feet. "I have not succeeded. All my labors may still amount to nothing. Nothing at all!"

A long pause was filled only with the wailing of the winds.

"Come. I will show you more."

The great globe glided forward into the curling mists. Behind them, the glowing cloud tree reached out its longest branch, as if it were trying to deliver a message to them before they departed. Gracefully it stretched, unfurling like a fiddlehead fern in the spring sunshine, until it was about to touch the surface of the globe.

With a sudden jolt, the globe accelerated its flight. The misty finger reached out to its maximum length, but fell a few inches short of its mark. As the unknowing voyagers vanished into the billowing clouds, the illuminated tree seemed to shrug sadly and recoiled its branch. Slowly, twig by twig, the luminous form went dark, until at last its light was completely gone.

"We're descending," Grandfather declared. "We must be approaching the surface of the star."

Just then a gigantic tower of flame, white at the center and red along the edges, arched above them in a burst of brilliance reaching thousands of miles into space. The atmosphere sizzled and sparked. It felt as if they had just flown into a celestial furnace. For an instant, the swirling clouds turned into scarlet flames, licking at the great globe and its passengers. Then, like a collapsing building, the titanic tower of flame fell back to the star. It washed over them in an avalanche of fire.

"Whew!" said Kate as the flames disintegrated and were replaced by deep red clouds. "I thought the desert on Nel Sauria was hot. This is definitely no place to have a real body. Even inside a globe. If we were made of skin and bones there'd be nothing left now but two lumps of charcoal!"

"Not even that," corrected Grandfather. "It's hard to believe, but we are only at the edge of the corona, Trethoniel's outer atmosphere. Compared to what it's like down inside the core, an eruptive prominence like that is barely lukewarm. The pressure in there is something like five hundred *billion* times the pressure on the Earth's surface, and the temperature is close to seventy *million* degrees Fahrenheit."

"That's what I call hot," agreed Kate. "It makes even a healthy Sun seem pretty feeble."

Grandfather nodded, as the globe drew closer to the turbulent, bubbling surface of the star. Bridges of superheated plasma, arching along the lines of magnetic fields, spanned gigantic cones of ejecting gas. Rumbling like countless engines, huge convection cells—seething pots of ionized gases—percolated with energy from deep within the star's core. The face of Trethoniel looked like one gigantic firestorm, continuously flaming, churning, and erupting.

"Look!" cried Kate. "What's that?"

They trained their vision on a great pillar of yellow-red flames that rose like the stalk of a fiery flower from the stormy surface. Upward it climbed, until finally it opened into a wide bowl, large enough to contain a planet the size of Jupiter.

As the globe approached the midsection of the gigantic flaming stalk, it veered to the side and began to spiral higher and higher. At last, they had climbed to an altitude where they could see the thick folds of red and yellow petals that lined the underside of the great bowl, shielding its contents from the stormy surface of the star.

"I wonder what it holds," said Kate.

"Something very special, I suspect," Grandfather replied, his voice filled with anticipation. "I didn't see anything like this when I flew near the surface with Orpheus."

"Could it be something that could help the Sun?"

"Possibly."

"Look!" cried Kate as they crossed above the rim. "Look at all those rows of bright green! But what—hey! What's that?"

As they flew above the fiery bowl, dozens of flat yellow creatures that glowed strangely became visible against the scarlet red background of the interior floor. The creatures glided busily to and fro across the radiant green rows lining the bowl, like farmers tending a fertile field.

Grandfather shook his head in amazement. "Those beings are huge! I would guess each one is at least the size of France! What are they?"

"They are Celethoes," answered the Voice. "They live in only two dimensions, so they can be seen only from above or below. Most stars have a few of them, but only the greatest stars have more than that. And no star in the universe has as many Celethoes as Trethoniel."

"And what are they growing?" asked Grandfather, eyeing the luminous rows of green.

"Pure condensed light," thundered the Voice, allowing each syllable to reverberate among the clouds.

Anxiously, Kate squeezed Grandfather's hand.

"It is the rarest element in existence," boomed the Voice, "a substance every star needs to survive. With it, a star will radiate life-giving light across the heavens. Without it, a star will surely die and go dark forever."

"That's—" Kate began.

"Quiet!" commanded Grandfather. "Let me think. Your Celethoes . . . could they be making PCL by breeding some derivative of the hydrogen isotope? Something like deuterium or tritium?"

"A good guess for a beginner, Doctor Miles Prancer. But the pure condensed light they are making is not related to the hydrogen isotopes capable of nuclear fusion. Such primitive materials I have long ago abandoned. My pure condensed light, unique in all the universe, contains free photons, twin neutrinos, and properties far beyond your comprehension."

Kate watched the graceful movements of the Celethoes. They seemed to be spinning threads of glowing filament from their own bodies, then weaving them tenderly through the rows in a methodical manner. Tiny pinnacles of illuminated green dotted the endless furrows: fresh PCL emerging from long incubation.

"And your Celethoes," probed Grandfather, "are they your only source of PCL?"

"No!" declared the Voice. "Over the ages I have developed many other sources."

"Such as?"

"I have no desire to tell you," bellowed the reply. "Even if I chose to tell you, it would take ten thousand of your lifetimes to explain, and then you would still not understand me."

Kate bristled at the Voice's tone.

Grandfather, however, seemed unperturbed. "With so much PCL available to you," he continued, "how can you be in any danger?"

"Because," the Voice rumbled, "I need something else to survive—something more precious even than pure condensed light."

"What could that be?" asked Grandfather, quite puzzled.

"In time!" roared the Voice. "I shall tell you when I am ready, when you will learn how to help me. But do not expect me to explain all my secrets to lesser beings like yourselves. I do not have time, and your tiny mortal minds could never comprehend more than a fraction of my creation."

Kate tried to contain her rising pique, but her thoughts betrayed her. "Who says we're lesser beings? Just because we might live for a shorter time. Aren't we all part of the same big Pattern?"

"Fool!" bellowed the Voice, with such force that the globe jolted and both Kate and Grandfather fell to their knees. "Contemptible fool! I do not need to listen to your childish babble. Trethoniel is the only place of perfection in all the universe!"

Grandfather squeezed her hand urgently.

"Forgive her, Great Star," he called into the mists. "She does not understand."

Kate's mind was whirling with images of The Dark-

ness, the terrible tail, the scorched desert of Nel Sauria
. . . These were not her idea of perfection. Why didn't
Grandfather understand?

"But—" she objected meekly.

"Not now, Kaitlyn!"

"Silence!" commanded the Voice, barely suppressing
its rage. "I tolerate her ignorance only because she trav-
els with you, Doctor Miles Prancer."

Kate cast a frightened look at Grandfather. Then her
eyes fell to the fiery bowl below them.

Something had changed. By some silent command,
the Celethoes had ceased in their labors. They were gathering together in the center of the red valley, their bodies
glowing brightly as they slid across the fields to their
destination. There, they formed a circle, a circle of connected light.

"The perfection of Trethoniel is under attack," the
Voice rumbled. "Ignorant Celethoes may continue to
perform their labors, hiding the impending tragedy from
even themselves, but that does not alter the essential
truth. Unless something is done swiftly, unless I can ob-
tain the one thing I need, the greatest star in the universe
will soon produce no more light and no more music."
There was a somber silence before the Voice uttered its
final sentence. "Trethoniel is about to die."

As the words echoed across the starscape, all fell still.
Even the wailing wind seemed to hold its breath as the
phrase *about to die* hung heavily upon it.

Then came another sound, subtle and struggling to be
heard. Faint though it was, Kate recognized it immediately.

"The music!"

The unmistakable chords rose delicately to them, like

the scent of a distant lilac bush on a gentle breeze. Harmonious was the song, and full of healing. Joyful, and full of peace. As Kate drank in the lovely music, she heard something which had eluded her before. Pain too ran through the melody, and tragedy as well. Yet, on some deeper level, the joy seemed to embrace the pain, as the peace accepted the tragedy. The power of the music was all the more profound because of it.

"The music—it's coming from the Celethoes!" cried Kate. She pointed to the shining circle below them, which seemed to swell in luminosity as the music swelled in strength. "They're trying to tell us something. I know they are. I can feel it."

Then a sudden turmoil filled the air. Kate caught a glimpse of a dark form gathering in the faraway mists.

"The Darkness!" she screamed in panic. "It's The Darkness!"

Just then she felt the terrible coldness reaching into her. An evil energy, even more powerful than before, began squeezing her tightly.

"H-help!" she gasped, reaching frantically for Grandfather's outstretched arm. "I'm being str-strangled!"

"Away with you," thundered the Voice. "Leave her alone!"

The music grew dimmer as did the circle of light below them, until finally both were extinguished. Heavy clouds surrounded the great globe, and the sky darkened ominously. The serpentine form of The Darkness encircled them, drawing its vengeful noose of anti-light tighter and tighter.

"Save us, Trethoniel!" pleaded Grandfather. "Get us out of here!"

But the great globe did not move. Only the muffled

groans of the Voice came struggling back from beyond the clouds.

Fear flooded Kate as she fought to breathe—desperately forcing herself to inhale. "I want to live," she sputtered with all her remaining strength.

The cold pressure inside her chest only increased. It was closing in on her, suffocating her, squeezing the life out of her heartlight.

Now The Darkness was circling so close that Grandfather could see the electric red eye, sizzling with currents of negative energy.

"Leave her alone!" he cried.

Kate coughed uncontrollably. Her hands grabbed her own throat, and she fell to her side, wrestling with an unseen force. She couldn't breathe at all.

Then, suddenly, she went completely limp.

"Stop!" screamed Grandfather as he scooped her into his arms. "Leave her alone, whatever you are!"

The entire sky flamed brightly, then went totally dark. At the same instant, Grandfather felt Kate's unconscious form disintegrate into nothingness. His arms were empty.

"Kate!" he cried, tears streaming down his face. "Where are you?" He groped madly in the blackness to find her.

In time, a dim light returned to the starscape. The Darkness had vanished, and so had Grandfather's last shred of hope. He collapsed in a heap in the center of the great globe, weeping bitterly.

Kate was gone.

14

the promise

KAITLYN, dear Kaitlyn," the old man sobbed. "Why did you have to follow me? Why did I ever make two rings? Oh, my dear, dear child . . . I am sorry."

With utter finality, three weighty words thundered across the clouds. *"She . . . is . . . lost."*

Grandfather slowly sat upright. He wiped his tear-washed face with his sleeve, struggling to regain a measure of composure. "What? What did you say?"

"She is lost," rumbled the reply. "Her heartlight has been extinguished."

"Extinguished!" cried Grandfather. "No! God, no!"

He placed his face in his two weathered hands. "It should have been me. Not her. Not my little Kaitlyn."

"Doctor Miles Prancer," spoke the Voice, "do not despair."

He raised his sorrowful head. "Do not despair? But

I've lost her. The person I most loved! Nothing else in the universe matters to me now."

"Something else matters. You also love the star Trethoniel."

A white eyebrow lifted. It struck Grandfather that the Voice sounded different than it had before. It was smaller, thinner, as if it had just survived a brutal battle.

"You love Trethoniel very much. And Trethoniel can still be saved."

"I can't think about anything but Kate," said Grandfather, shaking his head sadly. "Why didn't you save her? Why didn't you save her before she was lost?"

"I tried to save her. But I could not." The sky darkened slightly. "The Enemy wanted her badly. And the Enemy is very, very powerful. Never have I fought so hard, Doctor Miles Prancer. But I failed to save her."

"Who took her away? Who is the Enemy?"

"The agents of the Enemy are all around us. They come in many forms, sometimes frightening, sometimes pleasing. Deception is their weapon and destruction is their goal."

"Why?" cried Grandfather desperately.

"Because the Enemy is bent on destroying every star, every source of light in the universe."

"Including the Sun?"

"Including the Sun."

"But why did they want Kate?"

"She wanted the stars to survive! She wanted your Sun to live, and she wanted Trethoniel to live. Despite her vast ignorance, she was on the side of life, not death. She wanted my music to live, and to live forever."

"They can't have her!" protested Grandfather, tears again brimming in his eyes.

"They already have her," answered the Voice, some of its former strength returning. "They already have your Sun. But they do not yet have Trethoniel."

"Nothing else matters, now that Kate is gone."

"All life matters," the Voice replied. "And no life matters so much as the great star Trethoniel."

"Yes, of course, all life matters," said the old man halfheartedly. "But now that Kate is gone—"

"There is still time," roared the Voice. "There is still time to save the star you most love. But we must act together. And we must act swiftly."

Grandfather bowed his head in despair. "Nothing has any meaning for me anymore. Not even helping Trethoniel."

"Then do it for her. Do it for the young one. She wanted the music of Trethoniel to survive, to ring forever throughout the heavens. Helping me is helping her."

Slowly, the white head lifted. Clumsily, Grandfather regained his feet. His eyes were filled with sadness, but that sadness now mixed with his rising rage.

"Can we still stop the Enemy from destroying Trethoniel?"

"Perhaps," came the thunderous reply. "If we act now."

Grandfather's anger distilled into determination. "What can I do? How can I help you?"

For a long moment, the winds were utterly silent.

"You can lend me something," boomed the Voice.

"What can I lend you?"

"You can lend me your heartlight."

Grandfather winced, as if he had been struck by some object. "My—my heartlight? Great Star, you of all beings know that heartlight cannot be loaned! It can only be given, as an act of free choice. But once given it can never be returned. My heartlight would belong to you forever."

The winds whistled ominously.

"You are correct."

"But you're asking me—"

"—to make the greatest sacrifice any mortal being can make. Yes! To give up your individual heartlight forever. There is only one purpose that can justify such a request: the purpose of saving Trethoniel."

"So the precious substance you need is heartlight!" exclaimed Grandfather.

"Yes," answered the Voice. "A small dose of heartlight is the one thing I need, the one thing I lack. And I must have it soon, or the Enemy will destroy me."

"But I don't understand, Great Star! How can my heartlight be so important to you? Why is a little heartlight so much more necessary to your survival than all the PCL you are manufacturing?"

"Because," rumbled the Voice, "pure condensed light only prolongs life, while heartlight—heartlight is life itself. Pure condensed light has strengthened my body, but the darkest danger I face is to my soul. And the danger is upon me. Only heartlight can save me now."

"But why?" pressed Grandfather. "I still don't understand."

"You need only understand one thing." The Voice sounded closer, almost on top of Grandfather. "Trethoniel is now balanced on the thinnest edge of extinction. There is very little time left. All my beauties and marvels, all my music and light, will be destroyed forever— just like the young one—unless you help me. Even now, the Enemy is gathering for a final attack. You can make the crucial difference, Doctor Miles Prancer."

"Tell me more."

"I will tell you only what you need to know," replied the Voice. "The only fact you need to comprehend, which you have already guessed, is that I have labored for eons with all my energies to postpone the ultimate tragedy: that thing called death."

A swell of sympathy began to rise in Grandfather. "I know, Great Star. For so many years I have believed you were on the verge of collapse! How you have avoided it for so long is a miracle." He shook his head dismally. "I can understand your desire to live, to complete your work. You simply want to grow older and wiser, to avoid becoming—"

"—*a black hole*," roared the Voice, and with those words a new layer of darkness descended. "The Infinite Nothing! For eons I have lived in fear of this fate. The more beautiful I grew, the more inescapable it became. I have struggled in vain to avoid it, to find the solution to the terrible flaw that afflicts all living things. But I will struggle no longer. For I have finally discovered the answer to the greatest of all riddles. And I need only one more modicum of heartlight to complete my plan."

"So my heartlight will enable you to continue postponing your death?"

"No!" bellowed the Voice. "Postponement alone would be no success! No success at all! In the end, death would still triumph. No, Doctor Miles Prancer, I do not seek merely to postpone death, like every other living thing in the universe. I seek something far more precious. I seek to avoid death completely."

"Avoid death completely!" Grandfather's eyes opened wide. "That's—that's incredible! That would revolutionize astrophysics . . . as well as philosophy and religion! It would change everything!"

"Yes! I have labored for eight billion years to arrive at this moment."

"Perhaps," mused the astronomer, "my own life's work, brief though it's been, has also been just a preparation for this moment."

"And perhaps the young one's sacrifice was a necessary part of your preparation," added the Voice.

Grandfather jolted. "No! There was no purpose to that—no purpose at all! I would rather have her back than all the stars in the universe. She was lost out of stupidity—my stupidity—and nothing could ever justify it."

"I understand your grief," the Voice replied. "But our time is slipping away! Surely you are wise enough to understand what is at stake here. It is nothing less than the ultimate battle of the universe: the battle between life and death. Even the young one understood that much! Now, we have dallied long enough. Will you give me your heartlight?"

"If you first tell me how it will enable you to avoid death completely."

"Time is wasting! I could not possibly explain it to you in the time we have left. Nor could you understand the answer!"

"But I must understand at least a little more before I can give up my heartlight forever. It's such a final thing you are asking."

"Far less final than death! If you will not listen to me, then perhaps you will listen to someone else. Someone whose voice you will recognize."

"Who is that?"

All went silent, even the incessant howling of the winds.

"Who?" demanded Grandfather.

"It is I," declared a thin, raspy voice from behind the curtain of clouds.

Grandfather shook his head in disbelief. "No—it can't be!"

"But it is."

"Ratchet!"

A hoarse laughter echoed among the mists. "You look much worse for wear, Prancer. Yet still you made it here. Only fifty years late, but at least you made it. I confess I thought you never would."

Grandfather stood awestruck. "How did you do it?"

"How?" rasped the voice of Ratchet. "You are asking me how? The same way you did it, of course! Through a catalyst of PCL. Does it gall you to know that you were not the first to do it? That you were merely a follower, not a discoverer?"

"Yes," replied Grandfather. "Yes, it does."

"I see you haven't learned much, Prancer. You are as honest as ever."

"And you are as spiteful as ever."

"That is the prerogative of the greatest scientist who ever lived."

"So the whole fire in the laboratory was just a ruse?"

"To disguise my exit," agreed Ratchet, cackling proudly. "I am sure there was ceaseless debate over its true cause."

"Yes. But none of us ever guessed that you had found a way to free your heartlight and travel to Trethoniel."

"Or, even better, that I had discovered the path to immortality!"

Grandfather's eyebrows lifted to their maximum height. "You mean that you have merged your heartlight with Trethoniel's?"

"Yes!" Ratchet's voice was triumphant. "At last, to leave my wretched and decaying body behind. To be free, finally and forever! That is my reward for those many years of torture."

"So you have ceased to exist as an individual being?"

"What value is individuality when it is, by its very nature, limited and temporary? Now I am part of something much bigger and far better: the infinite life of a glorious star. And my great intelligence has enabled this star to flourish when it otherwise would have died."

"Fool!" bellowed the Voice, ending its silence. "You are only a tool to Trethoniel! I am growing tired of your endless arrogance. You forget that I have preserved a portion of your ego solely so that you can be more useful to me. But you have served your purpose! However important you might have been once, now much more important is your student. He alone holds the power to save Trethoniel from annihilation."

"Only because he learned a few things from me," snarled Ratchet. "And you have certainly changed your tune, O Voice of Trethoniel! You sent me all the way back to Earth just to prevent him from coming here! Now you are begging him for help."

"Prevent me!" exclaimed Grandfather. "Ratchet! Was that you who ruined my laboratory?"

"You've only now deduced that? You haven't gotten any smarter since I saw you last." Ratchet's hoarse laughter rose above the winds. "I actually quite enjoyed being a ghost."

"You might have killed my dog, you assassin."

"I wish I had. If there hadn't been more important matters to tend to—"

"Important!" Grandfather retorted angrily. "Like stealing an empty, worthless box! I do say, Ratchet, you are easily fooled. You haven't gotten any smarter since I saw you last."

"Silence!" commanded the Voice. "While you two are bickering, my very life is slipping away. And your life as well, Doctor Willard Ratchet."

"Why did you want to prevent me from coming here?" demanded Grandfather. "Answer my question, or I will never help you."

"Because I feared you would be captured by the Enemy, and made to give them your heartlight."

"But heartlight can only be given freely," objected Grandfather. "I would never give them my heartlight!"

"They would have tricked you!" bellowed the Voice. "They will say anything and do anything to annihilate Trethoniel. Just as I need one more drop of heartlight to survive, the Enemy needs it to destroy me."

"Prancer," croaked Ratchet's voice. "It was my idea to prevent you! I figured you might be getting close to making your own PCL by now, if you were lucky. You were never very smart, but you always had more than your share of perseverance. I couldn't take the risk you might be duped into giving your heartlight to the Enemy. And besides, what right do you have to make use of *my* invention? I was the only human ever to have experienced the power of PCL—until you had the audacity to follow in my footsteps!"

"Silence!" ordered the Voice. "I should never have listened to your foolish plans! It is clear to me now that your former student is far too intelligent to fall under the sway of the Enemy. And what is more important, I see now that he was destined to help Trethoniel in my moment of greatest need."

The Voice paused, gathering all its energy. "Doctor Miles Prancer, I have been joined by the heartlights of many wise beings throughout my realm. Now there are no more heartlights within my reach who have not sided either with me or with the Enemy. Your heartlight is therefore my only hope! Unless you join me very soon, the forces of the Enemy will triumph—and all my magnificence will be lost forever. I ask you now: Will you do your part to save Trethoniel?"

"What about saving the Sun, too?" asked Grandfather. "If I help you, will you give the Sun some of your pure condensed light? Its supply is dwindling fast."

"It is too late to save your Sun," declared the Voice. "But Trethoniel still has a chance to survive! And if Trethoniel can be saved, it will open the door to a universe where every star can live eternally, ascending to the heights of glory that stars were meant to achieve!"

A sudden pang of doubt struck Grandfather. "A universe where every star can live eternally? But what happens to the recycling of energy? What happens to the conservation of—?"

"Prancer!" cried Ratchet's raspy voice. "Have you not moved beyond those simplistic laws of physics? You were a fairly good student. Now you're sounding like a brain-dead Neanderthal. Don't you understand that immortality is within your grasp?"

"Yes, but—"

"We need your heartlight, not your questions!" interrupted the Voice. "You could not save the young one, and you could not save the Sun, but you can still save

Trethoniel! And in doing so, you will save the heartlight of many others as well. Will you join us?"

"Say yes!" urged Ratchet.

Straightening his tall frame, Grandfather peered into the impenetrable mists swirling about the great globe. He could not even see the outlines of the fiery bowl below, let alone the circle of Celethoes, if they were still there.

"I am prepared to help you, but only on one condition."

"I do not accept conditions from lesser beings," thundered the Voice.

"Then I will not help you," came Grandfather's clear reply.

"What is your condition?" demanded the Voice impatiently.

"That if any of Kate's heartlight has somehow survived, even if it is many eons before she is discovered, you will promise to return her safely to the planet of her choice."

"Nothing at all will survive unless you help me!" exclaimed the Voice with a force that shook the globe and nearly knocked Grandfather over backward.

"And I will not grant you my heartlight unless you accept my condition," he called back into the churning clouds. "While I still have my free will, that is what I demand."

"She has been extinguished!"

"Nevertheless."

"This is nonsense!"

"Nevertheless," insisted Grandfather. "I want your promise."

"Did you travel all the way here and leave your mind

behind?" derided Ratchet. "Why don't you join us?"

"I only know that if my heartlight is to be given away, it must be given freely. And before that can happen, I must have Trethoniel's promise."

"Very well," agreed the Voice at last. "You have my promise!"

The old man raised his hand to look at the remains of his lusterless butterfly ring. Only a small portion of one wing remained; before long, nothing more than a turquoise band would be left. "Once there were two of these," he thought sadly. "Now only one is left. What do the laws of physics matter if I can help stop the forces that destroyed her?"

"We must act!" roared the Voice. "Will you join us?"

"Join us, Prancer!" called Ratchet. "Make a decision for once!"

The winds swirled about Grandfather.

"I will help you," he declared at last. "I will do as you wish."

15

apple cider

"WHAT happened?" cried Ariella. "Why is there so much pain in the air?"

Her mother waved one of her long arms. "Quiet, Ariella! Go back to sleep. We are working very hard."

But the young snow crystal could not sleep. Something important was happening. She could feel it. She rubbed her round eyes and poked her head out of the pouch on her mother's back.

"It's so dark out here," she exclaimed. "Where has all the light gone?"

"Our light has been dimmed," answered her mother in an exhausted voice. "And the light of our snow as well. We gave it up to save the Creature."

"The Creature?"

"Come see for yourself," said the Nurse Crystal.

"But please, Ariella, don't get in our way. We barely rescued it and we still have much work to do. Twice during the battle I thought we had lost it."

"And we may lose it still," added another Nurse Crystal who was bending over the Creature. "It remains very weak."

Ariella spun down one of her mother's arms and landed on the velvetlike floor of Broé San Sauria. So dark was it inside the crystal dome that she could only barely discern the green color of the dome itself. Cautiously, she moved closer.

The dim illumination of the Nurse Crystals' bodies cast a wavering light on the Creature, who lay sprawled on the floor. Attentively, they massaged the limp form, all the while singing softly.

"Kate!" exclaimed Ariella. "It's Kate!"

Her mother stopped her work. "Kate of the Ring?"

"Yes!"

"Are you certain?"

"Yes! That's her."

"Ah," nodded the Nurse Crystal, her silver eyes examining Kate closely. "That explains much."

"Is she going to make it?" asked Ariella, twirling closer to her side.

At that instant, Kate of the Ring opened her eyes.

"Where am I?" she mumbled.

"You are on Nel Sauria," answered a gentle voice.

Suddenly Kate saw the huge, hulking shapes bending over her in the half-light. She grabbed her throat in fright.

"No. Stay away!" she screamed. "You can't have me!"

"Don't be frightened, Kate. I'm here."

"Ari-Ariella? Is that really you?"

"Yes. It's really me."

"How did I—Where is—" Kate struggled to sit up, then collapsed backward.

"Oh, Ariella! It tried to kill me again."

"Just be still," whispered another one of the Nurse Crystals. "You are safe now. Do you feel anything yet in your limbs?"

"Y-yes," answered Kate, her thoughts still whirling. "They feel heavy. Almost numb."

"Is the numbness moving into your chest?"

"I don't know! What happened to me? How did I get here? Where is Grandfather? Where is The Darkness? How did you—"

"Hush, hush," said Ariella's mother. She gently stroked Kate's furrowed brow with the tip of one of her long arms. "We will have time for explanations later. Now you must rest, or all our efforts will have been wasted. You are still in danger."

"I'll stay right here with you," whispered Ariella. "Don't worry about anything."

The Nurse Crystal reached into a small silver satchel dangling by her side. Out came her cup-shaped hand, with a sparkling dew upon it.

"This will help you," she said, as she touched Kate lightly upon the lips. "This is the same dew we use to nourish our most fragile baby crystals, when they are so small that even a beam of light weighs heavily upon them."

Kate felt instantly warmer, deep inside herself. Gradually, her questions gave way to a feeling of quiet comfort. An image danced across her memory of curling up beside Cumberland in front of Grandfather's kitchen fireplace, birch logs crackling, firelight dancing on the wooden walls. The room smelled of autumn leaves and apple cider. She lay her head upon his flowing red coat, and felt the dog's rhythmic breathing and warm body beneath her.

Soon she was fast asleep.

16

the true music

"HELLO." Kate looked up, her eyes filled with sleep.
"Hello."

She sat up straight and called into the semidarkness.
"Who is that? Where are you?"

"Here," announced a small voice behind her. As Kate
turned her head, the voice broke into a sweet, lilting
laughter.

"Ariella!"

"Right," beamed the snow crystal, her six ornate arms
glittering. "I couldn't wait any longer." She laughed
again, like legions of little bells pealing.

Kate found herself smiling. How good to hear Ariella's laughter again! Then, like a steel trap suddenly
sprung, her thoughts returned to her own predicament.

"Why am I smiling?" she moaned. "Ariella, what happened? How did I get here?"

"You were saved by the Nurse Crystals."

"Saved from The Darkness?"

"Saved from annihilation." Ariella's voice was somber. "The Nurse Crystals said you almost didn't survive. They said it was the worst battle they have ever had to fight in all the eons they have healed the wounded and tended their young. To save you they sacrificed most of their own light . . . and until it returns, the green dome and all of Nel Sauria will remain in shadows."

"That's why it's so dark?"

"Yes. Before the battle, the Nurse Crystals blazed with light, and the green dome of Broé San Sauria radiated their energy."

"I remember . . . And all to save me?"

Ariella nodded. "And Nurse Nolora will never make any light again."

"Why, Ariella? Why? I'm just a visitor to this place."

"I don't know exactly why, but I am sure they didn't sacrifice so much without a good reason. They must have known The Darkness was after you. If The Darkness wanted so badly to extinguish you, then your heartlight must pose a great threat to its plans."

Kate sucked in her breath. All at once, the horrors of her struggle came flooding back to her.

"Oh, Ariella! It was terrible!"

The snow crystal twirled to her side and nudged her arm. "I know."

"Grandfather!" cried Kate. "I've got to get back to him. He's in trouble. I'm sure of it."

She braced herself and tried to rise to her feet. Suddenly she felt very weak and dizzy.

"Too much too soon," chided a mammoth snow crystal rolling toward them. "Sit back down again."

The command was unnecessary, as Kate's legs collapsed under her. She fell back onto the soft floor.

"Ariella," spoke her mother sternly, "I told you not to disturb her."

"But I was only—"

"She was only helping me understand what happened," interrupted Kate, her head still whirling. "She meant no harm."

Ariella's eyes glowed with gratitude.

"Very well then," spoke the Nurse Crystal. "How are you feeling?"

"Better, I think. Less dizzy now. But I'm still awfully weak."

The Nurse Crystal's six arms quivered. "Understandably, given all that you were battling against when we came to your rescue."

Kate reached out her hand, and a long, glistening arm stretched to meet it. The arm of the snow crystal radiated a soft white glow, and as it moved, thousands of tiny crystalline points radiated rainbows in all directions. The outermost tip touched Kate's middle finger.

"Thank you," said Kate softly.

"You are welcome," replied the Nurse Crystal. "We will miss our light, and the dear friend we lost, but you are out of danger. At least for the moment."

"Why did it want to kill me?" cried Kate. "All I did was point to the Celethoes—they were trying to tell us something—when suddenly The Darkness was right there. It surrounded us, then it attacked me." She shivered at the memory.

"It was not The Darkness who attacked you," the great snow crystal replied.

"But I saw it. I felt it!"

"That much is true," the Nurse Crystal agreed. "But

The Darkness is only a slave. You fought it once before, we learned from Ariella. However, your last battle was not with The Darkness. Your last battle was with its master."

"Its master? Who is that?" Even in the near darkness, Kate felt a shadow fall upon her as she asked the question.

"We dare not speak its true name. It calls itself many things, all of them false. Most often it pretends to be *the Voice of Trethoniel*."

"The Voice!" Kate exclaimed. "I knew something didn't feel right about it. I just couldn't figure out what. But it kept saying it spoke for the entire star. I was starting to doubt my own instincts—to wonder whether I was crazy to be so suspicious."

"Trethoniel has many voices," declared the Nurse Crystal. "Every living being that is part of this star or its planets, no matter how small or insignificant, has a voice of its own. My little Ariella has a voice, I have a voice, and even The Darkness has a voice. None of them can speak for the star. The Voice that pretended to do so only kept you from hearing the other voices. But it could not speak for them."

"What about the music? The beautiful music we heard?"

The eyes of the great crystal danced. "If there is any true voice of Trethoniel, that is it. For eons and eons, the music of Trethoniel has grown in majesty and meaning. Each new voice that was added brought a new measure of beauty, a new moment of wisdom, and the song of this star became the most exquisite in the galaxy."

The Nurse Crystal leaned back to face the dark clouds swirling above the green dome, and her eyes darkened as well. "Until the Voice grew to be so strong! Then it began to block out our music, just as it blocks out any competing voices."

"But the Voice said it wanted the music to survive," protested Kate. "It said it wanted to save the music from total destruction."

"How do you explain that?" questioned Ariella. "That doesn't sound right."

Her mother's crystalline body, fully twice as tall as Kate, shook with anger. "It isn't right," she declared. "The Voice does not wish to preserve the True Music of Trethoniel. No! The True Music is made of mortal voices, a chorus of Celethoes and crystals and creatures of all kinds, whose music is made wiser and deeper by their very mortality. The music of the Voice, which it longs to preserve, is utterly different. It is a thin and artificial verse that could stretch on forever, oblivious to the pain of death or the tragedy of transformation. Only by understanding the unity of life and death have we given birth to wisdom and hope. The music of the Voice is immortal, but dead; the True Music of Trethoniel is mortal, but ever alive."

The two young beings sat silently, absorbing her words. At last, Kate spoke again.

"What is the Voice, really? Where does it come from?"

The Nurse Crystal did not reply.

"Please tell us."

"The Voice is part of the star," the great crystal said at last, "just as the True Music is part of the star. Like the music, the Voice is the sum of many individuals, but those individuals fear death so greatly they would sacrifice everything wise and beautiful just to stay alive."

"They are very bad," observed Ariella.

"No, they are not bad individually. They are only bad collectively, when they have grown too strong—as they have in the realm of Trethoniel. Every living being, young and old, has an echo of the Voice somewhere in itself. That is the call of self-preservation, of survival. It is a good and healthy thing, unless it grows too powerful."

"As it has here."

"I fear so," the crystalline creature said sadly. "As the collective heartlight of Trethoniel grew more selfish, the Voice grew in power. We who should have known better allowed it to grow too strong."

"But how could you?" demanded Kate. "How could you ever let such a thing happen?"

"Because it happened very, very slowly, and at first it seemed to be more good than bad. As Trethoniel grew and evolved, propelled partly by its desire to survive, much great beauty was wrought. Crystals blossomed like never before, Celethoes multiplied, starlight flourished, and healing warmth flowed throughout the heavens. Trethoniel became one of the loveliest stars in the universe."

Just then the darkened sky above Broé San Sauria rumbled with thunder. The Nurse Crystal wrinkled her face in concentration, as if she were straining to hear something. Finally, the deep silver pools of her eyes fell directly on Kate. "Someone you love is in very serious trouble."

"Grandfather!" exclaimed Kate. "What is happening to him? Is he safe?"

"No," answered the Nurse Crystal. "He is in the greatest danger that can befall any mortal being."

"Then I must warn him!" Kate tried to stand, but dizziness descended on her like a torrential rain, and she fell to her knees. "How can I warn him if I can't even get to my feet?" she wailed.

The Nurse Crystal reached a glittering arm to touch her brow. "Soon you will feel better. Your strength is returning faster than I had ever expected." Then a new thought twinkled in her eyes. "I wonder if Nolora..."

She looked at Kate lovingly. "You will be on your feet soon."

"Soon isn't good enough! I want to help him *now*."

"First you must listen."

Again, Kate tried to stand, and again the dizziness drove her back. "All right," she said resignedly. "I'm listening."

The eyes of the Nurse Crystal filled with the pain of some distant memory. "Slowly, inevitably, the Voice's lust for immortality overcame all the good works. Before those of us who understood the deeper truths could rouse ourselves, the Great Trouble was upon us. The Voice had grown very powerful—so powerful that we could not stop it from expanding the star beyond its true size. We could not even stop it from destroying the planets nearest to Trethoniel as it grew larger and hotter."

A sudden revelation struck Kate. "So that's how the Bottomless Blue turned into a big desert."

"Sadly, yes," agreed the Nurse Crystal, her moist eyes glistening. "As the star has swelled, it has burned away Nel Sauria's once-glorious ocean. At the same time, it has softened our snows, killed our crops, and warmed our side of the planet beyond a sustainable temperature. The Great Trouble grows worse by the hour. Never again will those wondrous waves embrace our snowy shores; never again will the wisest of the Nurse Crystals pilgrimage to the High Waterfall to meditate upon those infinite blue waters."

"The waterfall!" exclaimed Kate. "Did the Nurse Crystals build a trail to the top of this waterfall?"

"Long, long ago," replied Ariella's mother, "in the days when even the Sage of Sauria was young."

"Why didn't you explain all this to me before?" asked Ariella.

The Nurse Crystal touched her lightly on her arm. "Because you are so young, my child. I was hoping to wait for a better time, a more peaceful time."

"Why haven't you tried to stop the Voice?" questioned Kate. "Why haven't you fought against it?"

"We have!" the Nurse Crystal answered. "We have fought with every ounce of our strength—every ounce of our heartlight—just to prevent the Voice from achieving its goal."

"Which is?"

"To live forever."

"But," protested Kate, "that doesn't sound so bad. I mean, lots of people want to live forever."

"Indeed," the Nurse Crystal said wistfully. "Most mortal beings would love to live forever. But they cannot, because that would destroy the Pattern."

"Why?" asked Ariella.

"Because the Pattern is an endless thread that ties everything in the universe to everything else. If any being tries to go on living forever, then it must steal its energy from someone else who deserves to live. This star has a time to die, just as I do. And if the Pattern is intact, a being who dies doesn't totally disappear from the universe. It merely changes form."

Ariella spun to her mother's side and looked up at her

with doubting eyes. "Do you really believe that? Do you really believe we just change our form when we die?"

"Yes, my child, I do."

"Then why don't I believe it?" the small snow crystal objected. "Death seems so very final—so very sad. Please don't ever die! I don't want you to die!"

"I know," said the Nurse Crystal, as she stroked the delicate arms of her child. Her silvery eyes glowed softly. "You are right that death is sad. Perhaps one day you will understand it is also something more. I pray you will be given the chance."

"I've got to warn Grandfather now," said Kate with determination. "I've got to warn him about the Voice!"

"That will be very dangerous," cautioned the Nurse Crystal. "Remember what happened before! Are you certain you are really ready?"

Kate frowned. "Could the Voice really have destroyed me completely if you hadn't come to my rescue?"

"No," answered the Nurse Crystal. "Its powers are not yet that great. At least some of your heartlight would have survived." Her round eyes opened to their widest. "But for you, being extinguished might have been a kinder end. Any elements of your heartlight that survived would have been utterly mutilated, beyond any recognition. You would have been afflicted with permanent pain and undying agony. You would not have remembered your grandfather, and he would not have recognized you."

A shudder ran through Kate. She turned to scan the sky above the green dome. The darkness had lifted somewhat, and a pale red light sifted through the clouds.

"I've got to try again," she declared, struggling to raise herself.

The great crystal reached down and lifted her gently to her feet. "Then lean on me until you have regained your balance."

The dizziness had disappeared, but Kate still felt very wobbly. She rested for a moment against the broad body of the Nurse Crystal, not yet daring to stand alone.

"If the Voice is so powerful, why is it so afraid of me? I'm nothing more than a tiny flea, compared to a giant elephant. And what does it want with Grandfather?"

"Only you can answer the first question. But as to the second question, the answer is clear. The Voice is not yet immortal. It is almost there, but not quite. The future of this star now hangs on the thinnest of threads."

The Nurse Crystal paused, her intricately carved arms glistening in the dim light. "The Voice has been held in check by an alliance of many beings, great and small, near and far. We prefer music to thunder; we prefer the living universe to a living body; and we prefer even death to eternal stagnation. We have mustered all our strength, as has the Voice, and we have wrestled with each other until we have finally arrived at a complete and absolute stalemate. If only one additional drop of heartlight joins with the Voice, it will tilt the scales enough to destroy the Pattern. But the heartlight must be given by a being with free will, or it cannot change the balance."

Kate was thunderstruck. "So that's why the Voice wants Grandfather! It's going to ask him for his heart-light!"

"It has already asked," corrected the Nurse Crystal as she cast a worried glance skyward. "And your grandfather has very nearly accepted."

"No!" objected Kate, taking a few halting steps. She turned to face the crystalline creature. "He wouldn't do that. He knows too much!"

"He knows many facts. But his great knowledge may obscure his own wisdom. He may not realize that if he sides with the Voice, he will destroy the Pattern. And something more. He will also destroy his own heartlight."

"What do you mean by that?"

The Nurse Crystal bent lower so that her hexagonal face was almost touching Kate's. "Once heartlight is given, it can never be returned."

Kate stepped backward. "That means—that means he would die."

"No, Kate. It means something much worse. His heartlight would be *lost*. It would pass out of the universe . . . forever."

"But I thought heartlight could never be lost!"

"It can be lost if the Pattern is broken."

"No," Kate protested. "We must stop him!"

"The Voice must move swiftly if it is to succeed. If it does not cross the edge into immortality very soon, it cannot sustain itself much longer. The natural forces of the universe—the workings of the Pattern—will eventually win out. If, however, it can manage to swallow one more modicum of heartlight, then it would break the bonds of mortality and the Pattern as well. It would become a gluttonous monster squeezing the heartlight out of every living thing in its path. Already, just to sustain itself until it gets the heartlight it needs, it is consuming more pure condensed light than even the Celethoes can produce. So it has started to siphon the pure condensed light away from other stars."

"The Sun!" exclaimed Kate in horror. "Is that what's happening to the Sun?"

"Yes. The star you call the Sun is one of those whose energy is being stolen."

"And Morpheus and Orpheus. The Voice stole their light, too?"

"No doubt. But while light can be stolen, heartlight cannot. It must be given freely. And if your Grandfather is not stopped, I fear that is what he will do. Then the Voice will have won, and the Pattern itself will begin to unravel. The Voice will continue to grow like a deadly cancer until it has, finally, consumed or destroyed every drop of heartlight in the universe."

"We must reach him. You've got to help me reach him!"

The Nurse Crystal's eyes darkened. "If you try to reach him, Kate, you will have to do it alone. We crystals lost whatever powers might have been useful in our battle to save you. We are powerless now to do anything more than to keep our own heartlights aligned with the True Music. I'm afraid there is nothing more we can do."

"Then there's no hope at all."

"Kate," whispered the small voice of Ariella, who was tugging on her hand. "I won't let the Voice do anything to hurt you."

But Kate felt no comfort. "I want to do something," she whispered. "But what? I can't fly to him without Morpheus. I can't reach him with my thoughts—he's too far away. And you're right: Look what happened the last time I got in the Voice's way. It almost finished me for good."

An air of despair crept over Kate like a heavy fog.

She felt small, powerless, and alone. Glancing at her butterfly ring, she saw that it had continued to deteriorate, despite having lost its luster. Now only a quarter of one wing remained! Soon, she realized, the ring would vanish entirely—and with it would vanish any slim chance she might have ever to see the Earth again.

"Are you sure you can't reach your grandfather with your thoughts?" asked Ariella.

"Even if I could reach him, what would I say?" She fought back her rising tears. "And he's so far away behind the clouds! Oh, Ariella, what can I do?"

A small voice spoke from her feet. "You can love him."

The words pierced Kate through. "Yes. I love him. And I would give up anything for him. Even my—"

"No," interrupted the Nurse Crystal. "We cannot accept your heartlight."

Her face fell. "But you said one drop of heartlight on the side of the Voice would tilt the scales. So if I give my heartlight to the side of the True Music before Grandfather—"

"We cannot accept it." The Nurse Crystal's eyes were deeply loving, but her voice was firm. "Your heartlight is your own, and it does not belong to this star. Our laws will not allow us to take it, even to save Trethoniel."

"But the Voice will take Grandfather's heartlight!" objected Kate.

"The Voice does not live by our laws," replied the crystal. "And the laws have an essential purpose. The death and new life we will experience if Trethoniel returns to the Pattern will be far better than the endless life the Voice will experience if it does not."

Suddenly Kate recalled the mysterious words of the

Sage of Sauria: *There are two kinds of death for a star, and they are as different as hope is different from despair.*

A painful realization then struck her. "If we somehow stop the Voice, then Trethoniel and its whole system will die, won't it?"

The Nurse Crystal's voice grew smaller, almost as small as Ariella's. "Yes. Trethoniel will die instantly."

"And everything that's part of it? This planet? You and the other Nurse Crystals, too?"

"Everything."

"But that's terrible! That means Ariella . . ."

"Yes," the Nurse Crystal answered, in a tone of voice that reminded Kate of the True Music. "All of us will die."

"But how can that be good?" she demanded. "This Pattern is crazy! How is that any different from being swallowed up by The Darkness?"

"It is totally different. The Darkness is the opposite of the Pattern, a creature made of negative energy that has grown as the Voice has grown. The Voice has used it as a tool, but what it does not know is that The Darkness is really part of itself, just as an arm is part of the body that bears it. And The Darkness contains the seeds of the Voice's ultimate destruction. Today, it is merely a slave; ultimately, it will grow so powerful that it will consume the Voice itself."

"So the Voice will finally end up in a big black hole?"

"No," corrected the Nurse Crystal. "A black hole still belongs to the Pattern. It may be unfathomably dark and deep, but it is still part of reality. The Darkness, by contrast, is negating reality. A black hole merely transforms heartlight; The Darkness consumes it."

"Isn't there any other way?"

The crystalline creature looked at Kate remorsefully. "Not in this universe. No, there is no other way. The Pattern is not crazy. It is only very difficult to accept. I cannot live beyond my time, nor can any other being. Not without robbing something else of life. Not without upsetting the grand balance. I have lived a full and beautiful life."

"And I have lived a beautiful life," said Ariella bravely. "Just not a full one."

"Dear child," spoke her mother as she plucked her gently from the velvet floor. "I pray your story has some chapters yet to be written."

The Nurse Crystal turned again to Kate. "You are fast running out of time, if you still wish to try to stop your grandfather. Even as we speak, he is preparing to give his heartlight to the Voice. Gather all of your strength, Kate, then finally decide whether you truly want to risk such grave danger to yourself. No one would ever fault you if you do not."

Nervously, Kate tossed her braid over her shoulder. "If the Voice is really stopped, will that bring the Sun back to health?"

"We can't be sure. But if the Voice can be stopped before the Pattern is broken, it is possible—just possible—that all the pure condensed light it has stolen could flow back to its natural home, wherever that home may be."

"And that would return the Sun to health?"

"If my guess is correct, yes."

Kate drew a deep breath and stood erect. "I've got to try. But what can I do?"

"You can try to speak to your grandfather," answered

the great crystal. "You can try to reach him, to talk with
him, to help him hear his own deepest heart."

"But he's so far away! I can't hear his thoughts at all
any more." Kate raised her troubled eyes to the dense
clouds billowing above them.

"Perhaps you have not listened hard enough," suggested the Nurse Crystal.

"All I really want is to be someplace safe with him
again," said Kate wistfully.

"I hope you will be one day. Right now, all you can
do is try to reach him, if you dare."

"I don't know . . . I don't know . . ." Again she felt
the sting of doubt and despair.

Ariella leaped from her mother's arms and hung in
the air, suspended before Kate's face. She twinkled and
gleamed like a miniature star. For an instant Kate wondered whether there could be microscopic worlds and
creatures living on Ariella, creatures as small in relation
to the crystal as the crystal was to the star.

Ariella's round eyes shone softly. "Trust, Kate. Trust
in yourself."

Then the memory of the Sage of Sauria returned, and
Kate heard again her final words: *If you trust in the
Pattern, you trust in yourself. And if you trust in your-
self, your voice holds all the power of truth.*

Bravely, she turned to face the spot in the darkened
clouds where she imagined Grandfather now stood.

17

grandfather's choice

GRANDFATHER studied what little remained of his ring. But he found no comfort, only the painful memory of the loved one he had lost.

"We must act!" thundered the Voice. "Will you join us?"

"I will help you," said Grandfather, speaking slowly and deliberately. "I will do as you wish. But first, I need you to answer just one last question. Before I go out of the universe altogether, I must understand. Forgive me, but I am still a scientist."

"What is your question?" the impatient Voice demanded.

"I am troubled by just one thing. If you continue to live forever, because of my heartlight—"

"And if you delay any longer, I will collapse and die! I will perish absolutely!"

"Yes, I know," continued Grandfather, thinking hard.

"Just answer this question, and my heartlight is yours. Tell me why, if you continue to live forever, is not your energy displacing some other life in the universe? If energy is conserved, not destroyed—"

"Nonsense!" boomed the Voice, with such force that the globe jolted and Grandfather lost his balance for an instant. "You are asking for a class in the last eight billion years of developments in physics. I cannot answer your question in the time left to us. We may already be too late!"

"Prancer!" scolded Ratchet's raspy voice. "Didn't I teach you to overcome your doubts in order to pursue the truth? Haven't you learned anything about the way science works? Put your questions aside. We will deal with them later."

"All right. All right. No more questions."

"You are very wise, Doctor Miles Prancer," said the Voice in its most soothing tone. "Great scientist that you are, you will appreciate the most fundamental fact of all. This is an issue of life against death! Do you side with life, or do you side with death?"

At last, Grandfather's mind was clear. "I side with life, Great Star. With your life and the life of my lost Kaitlyn."

He drew in a deep breath, and opened his arms to the swelling mists. "I am yours, Trethoniel! You can take my heart—"

"No!" cried a young girl's voice from far away. "Grandfather, don't do it!"

He dropped his arms. "Kaitlyn!" he called, tears filling his eyes. "Kaitlyn, you're alive! You're alive!"

"Yes, Grandfather! I am alive. Don't do it, Grandfather. Don't listen to the Voice! Remember the music we heard . . . That is the true voice of—"

"Stop!" roared the Voice, with a force that rocked the globe and sent Grandfather sprawling backward. "Do not listen to that voice! It is not her, but an impostor! It is the voice of the Enemy!"

"It doesn't feel like an impostor," objected Grandfather as he struggled to get back up. "It feels like Kaitlyn!"

"It is the Enemy!" bellowed the Voice. "It is the voice of Death! Do not allow your longing to obscure your reason! Give me your heartlight now!"

Grandfather's turmoil swelled until he felt like he would explode. "What do I do?" he cried into the churning clouds.

"Give us your heartlight!" commanded Ratchet. "Do it now!"

"Don't do it, Grandfather!" came the voice of Kate, shrill and urgent. "The Voice doesn't value any life but its own. It's destroying the Sun, just to feed itself."

"That is a lie!" roared the Voice. "Do not believe the Enemy! Give me your heartlight before it is too late!"

"DON'T do it, Grandfather!" cried Kate, straining to reach him telepathically. She leaned against the Nurse Crystal for support. "Don't—"

At that instant, she started coughing. The terrible coldness was coming back, creeping into her heartlight. She felt a dark and evil force reaching deep into her chest, squeezing, squeezing hard.

"What's happening?" screamed Ariella in fright. "Kate! Kate! What's happening to you?"

Smash! The great dome was rocked by a gigantic blow, like a terrible earthquake.

"The Darkness!" exclaimed the Nurse Crystal. "It's trying to break through the dome!"

Smash!

The terrible tail of The Darkness slammed violently into the dome, and the vibrations nearly knocked Kate and the Nurse Crystal to the ground. Pieces of jagged green crystal showered on them from above.

Then Ariella screamed in terror and pointed to the dome. The electric red eye was scanning them through a crack in the crystal.

But Kate did not look up. She was struggling with another foe—an invisible foe.

"Grandfather!" she choked, trying desperately to keep herself from coughing. "Follow your heart!"

She fell to one knee. "Follow the Pattern!" she cried before another spasm of coughing made her collapse to all fours.

"Grand—" she began, when another blow exploded overhead, cutting her off. A gigantic crack appeared in the dome, and the tip of the deadly tail began to probe inside.

Suddenly, Kate felt very dizzy. She couldn't breathe anymore without coughing. Her face was on the floor and the world was going dark.

With her last ounce of energy, she pulled herself back into consciousness. It was all she could do to send one final message to Grandfather. She was too weak to wonder whether it would ever reach him. She coughed savagely, then fell totally silent.

*   *   *

"GIVE me your heartlight before it is too late!"

"Don't do it, Grandfather!" called Kate, sounding weaker than before.

The old man was completely torn. "Dear God!" he exclaimed. "What should I do?"

"Grandfather!" cried Kate's voice, suddenly stronger again. "Give your heartlight to the star! Do as the Voice tells you!"

"Kaitlyn!" he screamed into the whirling winds. "Are you now saying I should give up my heartlight?"

"Yes!" came the response, clear and strong. "The other voice was just an impostor! I am alive, Grandfather, but not for long! Give your heartlight to the star and I will survive!"

Now Grandfather knew exactly what to do. "Trethoniel!" he declared. "I give you my—"

Then a different voice halted him.

"No!" cried another Kate, sounding much weaker this time. "That's not my voice. That's an imitation. Grandfather, please . . . Follow your heart."

With all his concentration, Grandfather listened to the competing voices. "Kaitlyn! Kaitlyn!" he cried, tears streaming down his cheeks. "Which voice is yours? Give me a sign!"

"Save me, Grandfather," called the stronger Kate, beginning to choke with coughing. "Save us all before it's too late!"

"Follow your heart, Grandfather. Follow the Pattern," pleaded the weaker Kate, now barely audible.

"Give us your heartlight now!" bellowed the Voice.

"Give us your heartlight!" echoed Ratchet.

"Save me! Save us all!" screamed the stronger Kate.

"Follow the Pattern . . ." whispered the weaker Kate.

Grandfather's face twisted in pain. He closed his eyes, trying desperately to concentrate.

"Save me! Save us all!" cried one Kate.

"Follow the . . ." began the other Kate, before fading away entirely.

Grandfather strained to hear the final words of the weaker Kate. But no more words came. He could hear nothing but the wailing winds. Then, in the far, far distance, he heard a small voice whisper hoarsely:

All praise to thee my Lord this night . . .

"Make your choice!" roared the Voice. "Make it now!"

The winds screamed. Grandfather opened his eyes. He lifted his arms high above his head, and cried: "I choose the Pattern! I choose love! And I love you, Kaitlyn! I love you with all my heart!"

18

revenge of the darkness

A blinding flash of light seared the starscape. Thunder and electricity erupted everywhere. Crystals cracked, then dissolved into nothingness; mists sizzled and exploded with luminous lightning. The great cape of colored gases began to whirl about itself in a storm of devastating frenzy.

"Fool!" cried the Voice above the din. "Mortal fool! You have doomed us all!"

Wild winds lashed Grandfather. A floating crystal burst just above him, pelting the globe with flying fragments.

"Oh, my God," he moaned. "What have I done?"

"You have destroyed me!" screamed the Voice. "You have destroyed me and all of my works!"

"Prancer, you idiot," called the strained voice of Ratchet. "I sacrificed so much—and for what? For nothing! All because of you. You and that—"

His words were cut off by a wave of explosions that originated deep within Trethoniel itself. The raging surface of the star shook violently, sending blazing towers of fire in all directions.

"I can survive no longer," called the Voice, now barely audible above the great cacophony. "But if Death the Enemy takes me, it will also take—" A new wave of explosions buried the Voice's last words.

At that instant, the globe began to vibrate. The intensity grew and grew until it shook so violently that Grandfather fell on his side. Suddenly, it exploded into tiny pieces, hurling him into space.

"Hellllp!" His scream was swallowed by the shrieking winds.

As the clouds crackled with electricity, Grandfather spun madly downward toward Trethoniel. Helplessly he flailed as the forces of wind and fire tossed and bounced him. All about him the majesty of the star was disintegrating. Down, down he tumbled, faster every second, toward the seething surface of Trethoniel.

"Forgive me, Kaitlyn!" he cried.

A jagged blast of lightning ripped across the sky, illuminating everything.

Just then Grandfather glimpsed something breaking through the clouds. Torn by the angry winds, the object bobbed like a kite crafted of luminescent paper. Closer and closer it came, fighting vigorously against the storm.

"Orpheus!"

"I am coming!" called the butterfly, his powerful wings beating furiously.

With a swoop, Orpheus dove underneath him and gradually slowed his fall. Grandfather embraced the sleek, strong body and felt the rhythmic beating of the great wings, wings that flashed with the light of ten million prisms.

"Orpheus, you're back!"

The long antennae waved happily in response. "The Pattern has returned, and so have I."

Grandfather looked at his ring. The remaining slice of a wing was glowing again, pulsing with its old iridescence.

Another flash of lightning illuminated the starscape.

"Where is Kaitlyn?" cried Grandfather above the whirling winds.

LIKE a meteor, Morpheus sailed through the gaping hole in the great green dome that had once shielded Broé San Sauria from all intruders. As he scanned the scene below, he saw instantly there was no time to spare.

The Darkness had condensed its anti-light into a writhing body, whose blackness was broken only by the glowing red eye at one end. Slithering across the floor like a monstrous serpent of the void, it left behind the shattered bodies of three Nurse Crystals who had dared to stand in its way. Victims of the terrible tail, the smashed crystals lay in jagged pieces, their light forever extinguished.

Only one Nurse Crystal, Ariella's mother, still survived. Like a sturdy tree planted firmly in the soil of its birthplace, the Nurse Crystal stood as the last barrier between The Darkness and its ultimate prey: the girl who lay sprawled on the floor behind her. Morpheus realized with horror that Kate's motionless form lay completely unprotected, except for the lone Nurse Crystal and another much smaller crystal who was shielding Kate's face.

"Ariella!" cried her mother, not daring to take her eyes off the deadly tail that was coiling again to strike. "Get away from here. The Darkness will destroy you, just like the others."

"I won't go," answered Ariella. "Not without you. Not without Kate!"

"All we can do is hold off The Darkness as long as we can. If the Pattern has been restored, The Darkness will start losing strength. I only pray it happens soon— before we're all destroyed." Quickly, the Nurse Crystal glanced to the rear, and her deep silver eyes met Ariella's. "I love you, my child, and nothing will ever change that."

Suddenly the tail of The Darkness lashed out, and the air crackled with negative energy. At the same time, Ariella's mother stretched herself like a massive cloak, her long arms shielding Ariella and Kate.

Craaaack! With a searing explosion, the deadly whip came crashing down directly into the Nurse Crystal. She burst into pieces, sending up a flare of white light so brilliant that it stunned The Darkness momentarily.

The dark creature quivered for an instant, dissipating slightly. Then, with a flash of its red eye, it solidified again and started to coil its tail once more.

Morpheus blasted into battle. His wings accelerated to all-out speed, despite the injury from his last encounter with The Darkness. He would not be outraced again. Either this creature would know the pain of death—or Morpheus would himself.

The evil eye of The Darkness, sizzling with negativity, pulsed with rage as it prepared to strike the final blow. To the extent The Darkness perceived thoughts of any kind, it was unified and propelled by a single idea: revenge. Gathering every last shred of its destructive powers, the gargantuan tail coiled itself tightly for the attack.

Then the tail released, slashing through the air toward the helpless body of Kate. Ariella stood as tall as she could, stretching her arms wide as her mother had done. But she could only hope to shield a tiny fraction of the target.

Craaaack!

Morpheus flew directly into the evil eye, as an explosion of negative lightning ripped the air.

The force of the direct hit knocked the tail slightly off course, and it crashed to the floor just wide of Kate and Ariella. Chunks of green crystal fell from above, shaken loose by the impact.

The Darkness shuddered, as if a mighty sword had sliced through its brain. Then a wave of distant explosions, so powerful that they shook the entire planet of Nel Sauria, reverberated inside the green dome. The Darkness released a deep and painful rumbling, a sound so low it was beyond all pitch.

Slowly, the threads of negative energy binding The Darkness together began to loosen, and its body began to dissipate. The raging red eye flared in pain and then started to fade steadily, while a web of negative energy crackled around it. The tail, motionless at last, grew rapidly thinner.

Morpheus fell to the floor with a thud, his wings badly torn. Weakly, he crawled away from The Darkness and toward Kate.

At that instant, she opened her eyes. The first sight

she saw was the red eye glowing hatefully.

"Help!" she shrieked, rolling over to her side.

"You're safe now, Kate," said a familiar melodic voice. "The Darkness has lost its power."

"Morpheus! You're back!" Still groggy, Kate sat up and hugged the neck of the great butterfly. "I'm so glad you're here!" She glanced fretfully at the evaporating form of The Darkness and shivered. "Are you sure we're safe?"

"Kaitlyn!" called a new voice from high above her head.

"Grandfather!" she answered, seeing him sailing through the cracked crystal dome.

As Orpheus settled to the floor, the old man slid from his perch and ran to her. Kate quickly clambered to her feet.

"Thank you," whispered Grandfather, as he stroked her braid lovingly. "Thank you and bless you."

"You heard me," cried Kate happily. "You really heard me!"

"Yes," laughed Grandfather. "And so did the star."

Suddenly, Kate's eyes fell upon the hunched figure of Ariella, bending over her mother's shattered body. Instantly the joy of their reunion melted away. She pulled free of Grandfather's embrace and darted over to her.

Taking the weeping snow crystal in her arms, Kate viewed the ghastly remains of the Nurse Crystal who had restored her life—and her hope. For a while she said nothing, as her own tears mingled with Ariella's.

Gently, she set down the small crystal, whose soulful eyes were saturated with pain. "I'm so—"

Craaaack!

With a flash of negative energy, the fading tail of The

Darkness raised itself once again. Sensing Kate's presence, it slithered swiftly toward her, searing the very air as it moved.

"Run!" cried Grandfather.

Kate instantly leaped to the side, but Ariella, still immersed in her grief, did not move.

From out of the shadows, a small form rushed to Ariella and pushed her aside, just a split second before the tail smashed violently on the very spot where she had been standing.

Kate turned to see who had saved her. "Spike!" she cried, amazed to see him alive again. "It's you!"

The columnar crystal bowed awkwardly, due to the portion of his base that was missing.

"That's the bravest thing you've ever done," said Ariella, eyeing him thankfully.

"Let's not get carried away," he replied. "It takes a lot of bravery just to hang around you, even for a few minutes."

Ariella's misty eyes almost smiled.

At that instant, The Darkness crackled and stirred once again. Kate, Ariella, and Spike backed away quickly as the tail, now a thin version of its former self, rose straight up into the air. It hung there for a moment, swaying from side to side, as if it were shaking an angry fist at its conquerors.

Then it fell to the floor, leaving a thin trail of darkness in its wake. It lay there, quivering slightly, as it faded into nothing more than a transparent veil. For an instant, only the red eye of The Darkness remained, glowing feebly. Finally, with a sizzling sound, it disappeared completely.

The Darkness had departed.

Whether the creature of the void had truly died or had merely withdrawn to some other part of the universe, Kate could not tell. All she knew was that her heart leaped at seeing it go; all she hoped was that it had gone forever.

"We've got to leave, Kaitlyn." Grandfather's voice was filled with urgency. "The star has returned to the Pattern, and that means it's beginning to collapse." He looked at his ring: Only a small sliver of the right wing remained. It seemed to be disintegrating before his very eyes. "Let's go."

"But how?" cried Kate, seeing for the first time the tattered wings of her butterfly. "Morpheus! Your wings are ripped to pieces."

"Orpheus and I have already devised a plan," said Morpheus with a graceful swish of his antennae. "You and your grandfather will both ride on my brother's back."

"What?" exclaimed Kate. "And leave you behind?"

The antennae waved sadly. "I fear I won't ever fly again, Kate."

She stepped to the side of the great butterfly and placed her hand upon his neck. "I don't want to go without you."

"You must, Kate," Morpheus replied. "I will stay here with Ariella, who will remind me of the cartwheels I could once perform."

"But the star is collapsing," objected Grandfather. "If you stay here, you'll be destroyed along with everything else."

"I have no choice but to stay," answered Morpheus. He turned again to Kate, and his broken wings rustled like the leaves of a stricken elm tree. "I will miss you.

It was an honor to fly with you on my back."

"If only we had more time," said Ariella with regret. "Then perhaps I could find some way to heal you. But time is the one thing we don't have."

Kate stroked the black fur of Morpheus' neck. "I don't want to leave you."

"Come, Kaitlyn." Grandfather's voice was firm. He took her hand and helped her climb onto the back of Orpheus. Then he slid into position behind her, wrapping his arms tightly around her waist.

"Are you sure you can carry us?" he asked Orpheus.

"I can carry you," answered the butterfly bravely. "It is my grief that is now too heavy to carry." Orpheus waved his antennae toward Morpheus. "My brother, when will we meet again?"

The multifaceted eyes of Morpheus gazed at him somberly. "I don't know."

Through her swelling tears, Kate could see Ariella leap into the air. The snow crystal floated before her face and gently touched Kate's cheek with a single delicate arm.

"Ariella . . ." began Kate, but Ariella already knew her thought.

"I will miss you, too," said the shining snow crystal, her own eyes brimming with tears.

Suddenly, Kate removed her butterfly ring and placed it into Ariella's cupped hand. Simultaneously she reached for Grandfather's ring, which was on his hand at her waist, and grasped it firmly. As she had hoped, she remained heartlight because she was still touching Grandfather's ring.

"That's dangerous, Kaitlyn," said Grandfather sternly. "If you should let go of my ring while we're in flight—

even for an instant—you'll perish immediately."

"I know," she replied. "But I want Ariella to have my ring. Something to remember me by."

"Are you sure?" asked Ariella. "I don't need your ring to remember Kate of the Ring."

"I'm sure," answered Kate. "I want you to have it. Maybe—just maybe—it will give you a little more time. Maybe you can even find a way to heal Morpheus! Please take it."

"But Kaitlyn—"

"I want to do this, Grandfather."

Seeing she was unshakable, the old man shrugged in resignation. "All right, if you feel you must. But Kaitlyn . . . at least do this for me. You take my ring to wear, and let me hold on to you."

Kate studied him closely for a moment, then nodded. She took Grandfather's ring and slipped it on as he laid his large hand over her own.

Ariella clasped Kate's ring, her silver eyes sparkling. "I love you," she whispered. Then she dropped to the floor next to Morpheus and cried: "Farewell, dear friends! You have saved our star, now save yourselves!"

With that Orpheus began to climb. As they approached the splintered dome, Kate could hear the wild storm raging outside. She looked below to catch one final glimpse of Ariella. To her surprise, the tiny crystal was growing steadily brighter. As Ariella's radiance increased, she began to glow like a small star. Gradually, she grew so luminous that she seemed to be made more of light than of snow.

"I hope we still have enough time," said Grandfather.

Kate, however, wasn't listening. "I love you, Ariella," she said quietly. "And I always will."

19

the black hole

A devastating blast of supercharged lightning seared the sky. Crimson clouds billowed and the winds whirled about them with gathering fury.

"It feels like everything is falling apart!" cried Kate, as an octagonal crystal burst into pieces directly above them.

"It is," called Orpheus above the din. His antennae waved frantically, searching urgently to find his bearings in the swirling storm.

Boom! Boom! Boom! rolled the thunder of distant explosions, sending shock waves in every direction. Lightning sizzled through the starscape and brightly glowing gas was everywhere. Cannons of destruction sounded continuously.

Boom! Boom!
Boom! Boom!
Grandfather gripped the ring on Kate's hand ever

more tightly. Another bolt of lightning ripped across the sky. Crystals exploded on all sides.

Orpheus struggled to stay on course, but the stellar gale was intensifying. Furiously he beat his wide wings, pushing himself as hard as he could.

Kate watched the powerful wings laboring, as her worries mounted. What if one of these explosions knocked Grandfather's hand off the ring? Why did Orpheus seem to be slowing down?

The starscape flared with electricity.

"Grandfather!" she cried. "What's wrong with Orpheus?"

His face was ashen. "He is struggling."

"Against what?"

"Against the most powerful physical force in the universe."

"A black hole?"

He grimaced. "We may be too late to escape."

As the great butterfly strained to carry them forward, Kate realized that everything around them was being pulled backward into the deep funnel of darkness forming to their rear. Gas clouds, crystals, asteroids—all were being sucked into the center of the collapsing star.

"No!" she cried in terror, as Grandfather's description of a black hole flashed like lightning across her mind: *a force so powerful not even light can escape* . . .

Orpheus forged ahead with every ounce of his strength. His wide wings beat frantically, but his progress diminished steadily. Now they were hardly moving forward at all.

"He can't keep this up much longer. We're barely staying even. As the gravity increases—"

"Look!" shrieked Kate. "His wing. It's disappearing."

She pointed to Orpheus' right wing. The upper tip had vanished completely, as if it had been sliced off by a knife.

"My God! We'll never—"

Zzzzappp!

A sizzling explosion of brilliant white light crashed across the sky. So bright was the blast, much more powerful than anything they had seen, that it seemed to freeze everything instantaneously. The winds died, the wings of Orpheus ceased beating, and Kate felt she could not even blink an eye. Everything around them stopped moving, frozen completely, as if time itself had been suspended, and with it, the collapse of the star. The only sound they could hear was no sound at all: Pure silence surrounded them.

Suddenly, the luminous wings began to surge.

"We're moving!" Kate cried.

Grandfather shook his head in amazement. "I don't understand."

Orpheus flew swiftly, despite his sliced wing. They left star and storm far behind, still suspended in space and time. Soon they had passed the outermost wisps of Trethoniel's multicolored veil.

At length, when they had reached a safe distance, Orpheus glided to a halt. With a graceful swoop, the butterfly turned to face the star.

Trethoniel was bathed in a new illumination, a silvery light that glowed and shimmered. Something about it reminded Kate of Ariella's eyes. Then, welling up from the heart of the star, a beautiful sound came wafting toward them.

Floating in open space, they listened once again to Trethoniel's magnificent music. As the melody radiated

from the star, it felt—if such a thing were possible—
even more full and beautiful than before. The undertone
of tragedy no longer fought against the melody, but
joined it, enriched it, deepened it.

Then, as the music swelled in power, something mi-
raculous occurred. Very gradually, graceful wisps of
golden light began to form around Trethoniel, encircling
it in lovely luminescence. Pure condensed light. Slowly,
as if they were waltzing with the music itself, the broad-
ening beams of light began to undulate, twirl, then flow
outward into space. Forming great glistening arcs, they
stretched, like rainbows made of fiery filament, far into
the galaxy.

One of those luminous arcs, both Kate and Grandfather knew, would eventually reach all the way to the
Sun.

"You did it, Grandfather," said Kate softly. "You
saved the Sun."

The bushy eyebrows lifted. "No, Kaitlyn. You did."

Kate shifted uncomfortably on Orpheus' back. "I
guess I had something to do with it," she acknowledged.
Then she asked: "What happened back there? When
everything stopped so suddenly?"

"I've been wondering about that myself," he replied,
still studying the star. "Sometimes a collapsing star will
reach a point of temporary equilibrium that makes it stop
before collapsing any further." He grinned. "But that's
just ordinary physics. And I have a feeling that something more than physics was at work there."

"But how could it happen? I thought nothing in the
universe is strong enough to escape a black hole."

The old man's eyes sparkled. "I guess there is one

force in the universe even more powerful than a black hole."

"Look. It's collapsing again!"

With a flash of light, the star began to swirl once again in an ever-tightening spiral. Smaller and smaller it compressed, until finally only a tiny speck of brilliance remained. For an instant it glowed bright, then vanished completely, taking the music with it. Where once the realm of Trethoniel had graced the sky, only a point of impenetrable blackness remained.

For a timeless moment, they gazed in silence at the empty spot.

"Grandfather," spoke Kate at last, "do you think there's any chance—any chance at all—that Ariella could have survived? Maybe even Morpheus? Perhaps the ring . . ."

Gently, he squeezed her waist. "Only God knows the answer to that one, Kaitlyn."

"If they are gone," she said somberly, "the universe has lost some very beautiful voices."

Grandfather sighed. "Yes, they were magnificent. But . . . somewhere else in the universe, some new voices will be born."

"Do you really believe that?"

"Yes, Kaitlyn. For the first time in my life, I truly do." He placed his cheek against hers and whispered: "I believe that every living thing has a time to die, as well as a time to be born. That goes for stars, people, and chrysanthemums, too. The important thing is that they flowered beautifully while they were alive."

Something about his tone of voice was profoundly disturbing, and Kate instinctively placed her free hand upon his and squeezed. Hoping to change the subject, she said: "I think it's impossible to have an experience like this without it changing your whole life."

"That's right," he agreed. "Whatever kind of adult you might have been before, I think you'll be different now—just because you were foolish enough to follow me on a four-minute trip."

"I inherited a certain amount of foolishness from my grandfather, you know," she replied. "What do you really think I'll be when I grow up?"

Grandfather gazed thoughtfully at the wing of Orpheus, glistening in the starlight. Eventually, a white eyebrow lifted. "I think you'll grow up to be a wise and wonderful woman. A lot like your grandmother, as a matter of fact. You'll be a mother, and your children will love to hear you tell them about the stars. And—now I'm going out on a limb—I would venture you'll also become an accomplished meteorologist."

"A what?"

"A scientist who studies the weather, both on Earth and other places. What's more," he added, "your special expertise will be the formation of snow crystals."

Kate couldn't help but grin. "I love you, Grandfather."

The old man looked at her fondly. "I love you, too, Kaitlyn." He smiled. "And I always will."

Suddenly, Orpheus shook his antennae worriedly. "Our time is nearly gone," he declared. "If you wish to return to Earth—"

"Heavens!" exclaimed Grandfather, feeling only the slightest sliver of a wing left on the turquoise band. "The ring is nearly gone. Take us home, Orpheus!"

The great butterfly's wings burst into action, flashing in the starlight, as the old astronomer held tightly to Kate's hand that bore the vanishing ring.

20

chrysanthemums

As Kate opened her eyes, she found herself lying on the floor of Grandfather's lab. Smashed equipment, strewn papers, and broken bottles of chemicals lay everywhere; the entire place was in ruins.

Sitting up, she felt a dull pain throbbing in her head. *Must have been a hard landing. Maybe I hit my head . . .*

"Grandfather!" she called.

There came no response.

He's probably down in the kitchen. Making a new pot of tea or something.

At that instant, she heard a noise in the hallway. "Grandfather!" she cried.

Instead of Grandfather, a long reddish face with floppy ears appeared in the doorway.

"Cumberland!"

Before she could get up, Cumberland pounced on her. The retriever licked her face energetically, his prominent tail waving all the while. Then he started barking noisily.

"Enough, enough," she sputtered. "I'm glad to see you, too."

At last Kate freed herself from the dog's enthusiastic embrace. She clambered slowly to her feet. Surveying the wreckage of the lab, it seemed more and more strange that Grandfather wasn't anywhere to be seen.

It wasn't like him just to disappear like this, she thought, her uncertainty beginning to grow. It was almost like . . . like they had never left at all.

A pang of doubt shot through her. Was it all a fantastic dream? She rubbed her sore head again, wondering whether she had been knocked unconscious somehow. Could she have imagined the whole thing?

She stepped over a mass of twisted metal and glass that was once a laser, and with difficulty made her way to the door. Cumberland, who was already there, gave another loud bark. Then he turned and padded down the long hallway to the kitchen, limping slightly.

"Grandfather," called Kate.

Still no answer.

Increasingly unsure of anything, she followed Cumberland past the lengthy rows of bookshelves. As she entered the kitchen, her heart was pounding and she felt a mounting sense of dread.

She froze in midstep.

"Grandfather!"

There he was, seated in the old rocker. His white head leaned back against the chair and his eyes were closed. Both of his weathered hands fell limp to his sides.

"Oh, Grandfather!" Kate ran to his side and shook him by the shoulders. "Grandfather, please. Please wake up."

He didn't stir. Not even an eyebrow lifted in response.

"Oh, no!" cried Kate, kneeling by the rocker and burying her face in the faded picnic cloth that still covered his lifeless body. "Don't die, Grandfather," she wailed. "Please—please don't die."

For many minutes Kate wept, and the picnic cloth grew moist with her tears. "So it was just a dream," she sobbed. "Ariella and Morpheus and the Voice and everything."

She raised her head and looked sadly around the kitchen. How empty it seemed now. Her eyes fell to Cumberland, who was sitting by the rocker, nuzzling against Grandfather's leg.

She rubbed behind the devoted dog's ear. "There's nothing you can do to bring him back," she said dismally.

Cumberland turned toward her, and started licking her hand. Kate noticed for the first time that the cut on her wrist from the flying shard of glass had returned. The edge of her sweatshirt was stained with blood.

Then she saw what Cumberland was licking: Upon her finger rested a simple turquoise band.

Even in her grief, Kate's heart leaped. She reached for Grandfather's hand, the hand that had once worn the very same ring, the hand that had brought Morpheus and Orpheus into being. Tenderly, she kissed his hand, then placed it upon his chest.

She rose and walked slowly over to the telephone on the kitchen counter. Her ankle ached painfully, but the greater pain was in a place she could not touch. She dialed home; fortunately, her mother was there. All she had to say was the word *Grandfather*, and her mother knew something was dreadfully wrong.

"You just wait there, Kate, and we'll be right over. I'll take care of calling an ambulance."

"Thanks, Mom," she said, replacing the receiver.

Without any conscious thought, she walked past Grandfather's body and over to the kitchen door. She opened it and stepped into the chilly autumn air.

The sky looked gray and full of grief. Somberly, she shuffled along the flagstone walk in the direction of the garden. At last, she leaned against the old wooden gate, her heart heavy with loss.

There was the great stone fountain, and the patch of unruly grass where they had picnicked only yesterday. The chrysanthemums were still strong, but their colors seemed more muted than before. The grape arbor hung heavily, and the scent of its rotting fruit filled the garden. The air had grown colder and the sky darker.

Suddenly Kate felt a crisp breeze against her back. She glanced at the wintry clouds gathering overhead. It felt like the first snowfall of the season was about to begin.

Slowly, very slowly, a diffuse line of light stretched across the sky. With a strength as irresistible as the first sapling of spring pushing past the lingering snow, the line of light deepened and broadened. Then, with a flash, the Sun broke through the clouds.

Kate's gaze fell to a purple chrysanthemum. As she watched, a single petal dropped to the ground, spinning slowly as it fell.

The bestselling author of the *Lost Years of Merlin*
saga branches off in a new direction that
"will surely delight readers" (Madeleine L'Engle).

T.A. BARRON
Tree Girl

0-441-00994-8

A nine-year-old girl searching for her roots
must face a forest filled with tree ghouls—
and her own deepest fears.

"Sprightly, magical, and wise."
—Barbara Helen Berger